TAURUS: Some highs, but a very bad day overall. Watch out for arguments and avoid following bad advice.

He waited in the shadows once again. In the week since he'd taken Jenny Warren's sacrifice, he had been watching and waiting for the right moment to make his next move. Now was the time—the stars had spoken.

Life was a vast wheel, turning slowly behind the superficial mask that was shown the world. But he had seen the reality. He knew that the wheel of life and death was the wheel of the Zodiac. The stars had spoken to mankind, laid down their unbreakable laws. Most people had ignored it, but not him. He had heard the song, the music of the spheres, and he was an embodiment of the truth. He was one in purpose with the stars. He was their messenger.

Tonight, the message was death.

He fingered his star-selected weapon and smiled to himself. Tonight the second stage in the great wheel would be filled. In just a very short while.

Don't miss these other books
by *Nicholas Adams*

Horror High

#1 Mr. Popularity
#2 Resolved: You're Dead
#3 Heartbreaker
#4 New Kid on the Block
#5 Hard Rock
#6 Sudden Death
#7 Pep Rally
#8 Final Curtain

I.O.U.

Santa Claws

Also available from Harper Paperbacks

The Vampire Diaries
by L.J. Smith

Volume   I: The Awakening
Volume II: The Struggle
Volume III: The Fury

Horrorscope

Nicholas Adams

HarperPaperbacks

A Division of HarperCollinsPublishers

HarperPaperbacks *A Division of* HarperCollins*Publishers*
10 East 53rd Street, New York, N.Y. 10022

Produced by Daniel Weiss Associates, Inc.
33 West 17th Street, New York, New York 10011.

First printing: February 1992

Printed in the United States of America

HarperPaperbacks and colophon are trademarks of
HarperCollins*Publishers*

10 9 8 7 6 5 4 3 2 1

ONE

ARIES: Loved ones will be argumentative. Avoid confrontations. A bad day for relationships.

He waited silently in the shadow of the large elm. His eyes were fastened on a pool of light farther down the road. Beneath a street lamp was a battered Ford, its lights out. But they were in it, he knew. Jenny Warren and her boyfriend, Derek Vine. Let them have their fun for now. It would be his turn soon.

It was written in the stars.

In his hands he held a cheap red and white woollen scarf. The ends were wrapped around each palm, and the only movements he made were to twist the scarf, over and over again. It was all done subconsciously. His eyes never left the parked car.

He waited.

* * *

"Not again, Derek, okay?" Jenny sighed, her eyes closed, her head leaning on the headrest. "Give it a break."

Derek glared at her, irritated. Jenny was especially pretty right now, looking almost relaxed in the car seat. Her auburn hair framed her face and fell in light waves down to her shoulders. It was a warm spring evening, and her arms were bare, the top she was wearing being little more than a halter. She wore frayed jeans that covered her long, shapely legs. She really was one of the best-looking girls in school, and he still felt amazed that she had ever agreed to go out with him. There was only one problem—his mother. A staunch member of the First Apostolic Church of Fremont, Mrs. Vine hated the fact that her oldest son was dating a non-Christian.

"Come on," he tried again, willing to beg if he had to. He was working on controlling his temper; why was she being so obstinate about this, knowing how important it was to him? "It won't hurt you to try it just once, right? One measly church service. Hour and a half, forty-five minutes max."

"I said no," she replied coldly. "Non, nein, nyet. And that's my last word." She sat up and shook her head. "My horoscope warned me it was going to be a bad day."

Derek winced. Good thing Mom wasn't here. She thought horoscopes were positively occult. Jenny read her fortune daily in the newspapers. "I wish you'd give that up," he said.

"Oh, great!" Jenny glowered at him. "I'm supposed to do everything you want now, huh? Well, I've got news for you—I like me just the way I am. If you don't, it's time to get yourself a new girlfriend. Understand?"

2

Worried, he reached out to try to calm her down. She pulled back, then opened the car door. "I'm going home now," she told him. "You run back to Mommy and tell her what a lost soul I am."

"I'll drive you home," he mumbled, uncertain of how things had ended up so badly.

"Don't bother. It's only a few blocks, and my legs are in fine shape—as you should know." She got out of the car and slammed the door shut. "Good night!"

He rolled down the side window. "Jenny, please don't go."

She turned to look at him. The streetlight, shining through her halo of hair, made her look almost angelic. She sighed. "Derek, when you cut your mother's apron strings, talk to me again. Till then, I've had enough." Spinning on her heels, she strode determinedly into the darkness.

Derek sat in the car, staring into the blank night, his mind a jumble of emotions. He wanted to run after Jenny, but knew that would be futile. She was too strong-willed to back down after that ultimatum. He wanted to yell or pound on something, but that was just stupid. He wanted—well, he wanted his mom to get off his back about Jenny. That was very, very unlikely. The two of them simply rubbed each other the wrong way. Why was it that the two people he cared for the most couldn't get along?

Because they had entirely different systems of belief. His mother measured everything she or her children did by the standards of the Bible and her church. *Their* church, since the whole family went. Jenny didn't believe in any form of organized religion. She said it was

3

all a crock, an attempt to control the minds of the weak. As for him . . . well, he wished there was a middle ground, where he could accept his mother's faith without the burdens it seemed to bring.

Sighing, Derek started up the car. He wished he could go after Jenny, but he knew he had to go back home. He fully expected his mother to give him the silent treatment. Why couldn't she butt out of his love life? And why was Jenny being so stubborn? Would it really hurt her to go to one service and see how she felt afterward? She was being so unreasonable! Why did he like her so much? Maybe she would change, with time? He didn't know what to feel or where to turn.

And these were supposed to be the happiest years of his life?

He smiled, unseen in the darkness. As he had known, she was coming. Alone. Derek had left her here, for him.

All was as it was meant to be.

She had left the protective circle of the lamp behind and was little more than a silhouette in the night. She walked fast, her low heels clicking on the sidewalk. There were lights on in the neighboring houses, but the streets were empty.

It was perfect.

His hands fashioned the scarf into a noose again and he stood immobile in the darkest shadows. She was walking right toward his hiding place, oblivious to his presence. His stars had been right. The timing was perfect.

Soon, very soon.

4

He tried to quell the rising joy within, afraid that he'd do something foolish, like laugh aloud and scare her off. It was hard. With Jenny, it would begin. And it would end . . . well, not for a while yet. Jenny was just the first. Because of that, she was the most important. He had to do it exactly right.

The sound of her heels came closer and closer. Each second seemed to grow longer than the previous one, as if time was slowing down. He listened, carefully, waiting for just the right moment to—

—leap out from hiding. Jenny was suddenly aware of him and she started to turn, to open her mouth. But she was too late. The scarf was around her throat, and he pulled, tighter and tighter. He felt light-headed, vaguely surreal, as he applied the pressure, ignoring her struggles. The choking hold around her neck gave her no chance to call for help. He kept up the relentless pressure.

Then it was over.

He lowered her body to the ground and released his hold on the scarf. There was no movement. To be certain, he checked for her heartbeat, but there was nothing.

He had done it. He had killed her.

Just for a moment, he felt hollow. Surely there should be something? Some surge of energy, some excitement? Not this emptiness? Oh, well—this was only the first. Maybe the feeling of power would come later. Right now, he still had work to do. He regarded the fallen girl with a critical eye. Then, feeling more certain, he pushed aside the hair that was obscuring her face. He loosened the scarf around her neck a little, showing part of the bruised skin beneath. Then he took a couple of paces back.

Much better. Now she looked really dead, not just fallen. He cocked his head to one side, then the other. He moved around a bit, to get a better view of the body. Then, nodding with satisfaction, he pulled a camera from his pocket.

Lining up the body in the view finder, he took a photo. The flash seemed terribly bright, and he waited. There was no sound from any of the houses. He was probably safe enough. He took a second picture, just in case the first one didn't come out. Then he put the camera back into his pocket. He looked down at Jenny Warren's body one last time.

"Thank you," he told her gratefully. "You've been a big help." Then, feeling a lot happier, he walked off into the night, leaving the broken form behind him.

TWO

LEO: *The morning will bring unpleasant news. A decision will be made for you that you might object to.*

"Are you ready for school yet?"

Robyn Chantry heard her mother's voice from downstairs and examined her reflection in the mirror. Her hair—so red it was almost glowing—was still all wrong. No matter how hard she tried, it had a mind of its own and refused to be brushed into a neat style. Scowling at her image, she pulled on a yellow and green sweatband, forcing her hair to lie at least a little closer to her head. That done, she felt better. The long, green gypsy-style skirt and the lemon-colored blouse were pretty sharp. Her sandals were old and somewhat beaten-up, but very comfortable, which was what mattered to her.

Some of the kids at school made fun of her style—as if baggy jeans and faded T-shirts were a compulsory uniform. Robyn didn't really care what they thought. She had learned from her parents that it mattered more that she knew who she was than whether anyone else appreciated it. So a few of her schoolmates made fun of her. Big deal. They could go jump. She had her own crowd. And, if she was honest with herself, she kind of enjoyed being a bit of a rebel at school.

"Robyn?" her mother called again, a slight edge of impatience to her voice. "If you want a ride to school, move those feet!"

"Coming!" Robyn called, snatching up her tote bag and slinging it across her shoulder. Spot check of the room—anything she'd forgotten? The unicorn in the poster on the wall seemed to stare haughtily back at her. She made a face at it. The crystal suspended in her bedroom window sent its rainbow of light across the far wall, onto her Pink Floyd poster. She liked the older music better. After all, Fine Young Cannibals or 10,000 Maniacs were okay, but no one could touch the late sixties. The top of her desk was clean—no forgotten homework. And there was nothing on her neatly-made bed. She guessed it was all in her bag—judging from the weight of it, most of her room was in there, too. She smiled at the teddy bear dressed in wizard's clothing on her chest of drawers, and shot downstairs.

On the way out, Robyn stopped in at her father's studio. She loved the fact that both of her parents were as unconventional as you could get. Her best friend, Debi's, father was a banker—*borrrring*. Robyn's dad was much more interesting.

He was already at work, busily mixing up a batch of wax. His studio's end products—candles in the shapes of people, mythological creatures, castles, birds, and animals—were lined on shelves, ready for the final touches that gave them the semblance of life. Her father was extraordinarily skilled, and his candles were in big demand at craft shows, medieval fairs, and the S.C.A. events her parents never missed. In fact, there was a Society for Creative Anachronism event this weekend, and Mr. Chantry was busy making samples to take with him. Robyn had always liked going to those things with her parents. She knew some of her friends thought that dressing up in costumes and pretending they were living in the Middle Ages was kind of weird. Personally, Robyn thought that they just lacked the imagination to really enjoy it.

"Hi, Dad. Bye, Dad."

Her father looked up and grinned at her. His long, sandy hair was tied into a knot at the back of his head, and he wore a wax-splattered apron. "How's my best girl?" he asked, checking the temperature of the melting wax in his electric cauldron.

"Off to school," she answered. "What's cooking?"

"A couple of special orders. It's John and Fern's third anniversary next month, so I'm doing something fun for them. They don't know about it, so don't tell them. And I've gotten a weird order for a Vlad the Impaler piece."

"Doesn't sound like your kind of thing," Robyn said, frowning. She knew that Vlad was the bloody-handed tyrant who had inspired the original story of Dracula.

"It isn't, really. I'm not into dead bodies, blood, and swords. Still, it's for an old friend, and it's hard to turn him down." A car horn honked from the driveway. "Sounds like your mother's waiting. Bye, honey."

"Bye, Dad." Robyn dashed out of the house and into the passenger seat of the minivan.

"About time, young lady," her mother said, pretending to be miffed. "I almost left without you."

"Sure you did," Robyn said with a laugh.

Her mother snorted and started off. She was an older version of Robyn, with the same flame-colored hair—though in her case it was chopped off in a pageboy. "More manageable when you get to my advanced age," she'd told Robyn. "But when you're young, you don't care about all of the work that goes into looking beautiful." Despite that, she was still definitely pretty. Robyn suspected that most of the male customers in her mother's health-food store came in more to see the owner than out of a burning desire to eat healthily. Robyn sometimes helped at the store, and she always got a kick out of the men trying to date her mother—or even her. "Don't pay any attention to them," her mother always said. "They're only after one thing: free samples."

"Are we picking up Debi again today?" Mrs. Chantry asked, honking the horn as an idiot in a Toyota cut them off.

"Yeah. Her dad's car's still in the shop."

"Serves him right for buying a Jaguar," her mother answered unsympathetically. She couldn't respect people who bought status symbols. "But I don't see why Debi should suffer for his sins. But she'd better be ready, or else . . ."

Robyn smiled to herself. Her mother always made that threat, and never kept it. Besides, she usually kept *them* waiting while she chatted with Mrs. Smolinske anyway. She had a nerve to complain!

A few minutes later, they pulled up outside the Smolinskes'. They had a large, Victorian-style house, immaculately landscaped and very expensive. Two stone lions flanked the path that Debi was coming down. She waved hello to them. She was wearing a cream-colored top and black form-fitting pants. Her parents wouldn't let her wear T-shirts, jeans, or sneakers, considering them too common for their darling only daughter. Debi thought her parents were snobs, but she was stuck with their decisions in the clothing department. The Smolinskes were very conscious of their image in town, and were utterly inflexible when it came to having opinions. Debi brushed her long, jet-black hair from her face and smiled at Robyn as she clambered into the back seat.

"How goes the day?" she asked.

"For you or me?" Robyn answered. "According to your horoscope, today will be pretty good, especially in the afternoon. As for me, I'm going to have problems all day long. But there's no sign of any yet."

"You take this horoscope business much too seriously," Robyn's mother said, pulling out too close to a passing Mazda. "I told you, tarot cards are much more reliable."

Robyn shrugged. "I just don't feel the same affinity for them as you do. But I really feel the stars."

Debi sniffed loudly. "I think it's all a load of kitty litter." But she smiled as she said it.

"Oh, right," Robyn said. "And who's always first to ask about her own fortune?"

11

"I'm just being polite," Debi said with dignity. "I humor you."

"Sure." Robyn dived into her bag and sorted till she found the two sheets of paper she wanted. Fishing them out, she passed them over to Debi. "That's my latest column. I've got to meet with old Twinkletoes today—could you turn these in to Ms. Tepper for me?"

Debi glanced at the column. The heading read: MY STARS! BY JEAN STEPHENSON. Robyn had adopted that name for her horoscope column in the school's weekly newspaper. She thought it sounded more romantic and mystical than her own. Privately, Debi had never agreed. How much more romantic could you get than Robyn Chantry? But there was no arguing with her. "Okay. I've got a couple of pieces to drop off myself."

"What's this meeting?" Mrs. Chantry asked. "And who's old Twinkletoes?"

"Mr. Traynor," Robyn replied. "My science teacher. He wants to talk to me today."

Her mother looked at her, hard. Robyn squealed and pointed to the road. Mrs. Chantry resumed watching the traffic and said: "Your grades have been slipping, haven't they?"

"Well, he's so boring. And, anyway, I'm artistic, not scientific. It's the Leo in me."

"That's no excuse for not doing your best," her mother answered. "The stars don't make our destiny, you know—they just influence it." She signaled and pulled to a halt outside of the high school building.

It was one of those red-brick affairs, with ranks of uniform windows, a carpet of grass in the front, and playing fields to the side. To Robyn, it spelled boredom with a capital yawn. To avoid further lecturing, she slid out of the minivan and waved. "Have a good day at the shop." Debi joined her, and they watched the minivan draw away. Then Debi shook her head.

"You didn't give her that note from Twinkletoes?"

"It would only have set her off," Robyn answered. "She's a Sagittarius. She loves to lecture. Besides, it'll just be some stupid thing like me not understanding the theory of relativity or something. Twinkletoes just likes to hear himself talk."

Debi giggled. "Let's face it, he's the only one who does."

They headed through the main entrance, to their lockers. This was where the Gang of Four always met up before class. Dana Mullalley, Natalie Byrnes, Robyn, and Debi had been friends from first grade up—ignoring the occasional fight or two, which was usually forgiven and forgotten quickly enough. They had had so many sleep-overs that they had lost count. Now, of course, they had different interests and lives, but the looming threat of graduation was pushed to the backs of their minds. Surely nothing could split them up?

There were other students gathered around the lockers, but the usual laughing and talking was missing. Dana and Natalie looked around. Both were adopted Korean girls, and because of this, felt almost like sisters. They were vaguely alike, at least in features. Both were tall, with long, shiny black hair, and clear complexions. Normally, they were completely dissimilar in character, though: Dana was serious and attentive, while Natalie was frivolous and an addicted shopper. Today, though, both wore very serious expressions. Natalie looked as if she'd been crying.

Robyn looked at them, and then at the drawn faces of their other friends. "What's wrong?" she asked, finally breaking the dark silence.

"It's Jennifer Warren," Natalie said in a hollow voice. "She was murdered last night. And the police think that Derek Vine did it."

Robyn looked at Debi and saw her own horror, shock, and grief reflected in her friend's eyes. She slumped back against her locker, feeling as if she'd been stabbed through the heart. *Jenny—dead!*

And, worse—someone in their class suspected of doing it.

THREE

SCORPIO: Unjust accusations will cut you to the quick. Watch your temper, and avoid retaliating.

Derek stared at Sheriff Adkins and the nameless deputy who stood just inside the homeroom door. His arms crossed, the deputy was staring blankly into space while making sure that nobody else entered the room until the sheriff allowed it.

Sheriff Adkins was someone that Derek had known only by name before this horrible morning. His stomach hung over his belt, which was already on its last notch. Slightly balding, his gray hair slicked back, the sheriff stared at Derek. His dark eyes watching for—what? Guilt? A confession? Derek wished he knew, but the sheriff's impassive face gave away nothing.

Actually, all Derek wanted was to be left alone. The sheriff had broken the news about Jenny's murder and begun questioning him almost without pause. Derek felt like he had to be alone somewhere—to cry, or throw up, or something. Not Jenny . . . anyone but Jenny.

"Let's try it again," Adkins said softly. "You were with her last night, right?"

"I already told you that!" Derek said, a little too loudly. "Do you think I killed her? She was my girlfriend, for God's sake!"

The sheriff shrugged. "At this stage in the investigation, son, I don't think anything. I just ask questions. I want to get everything straight in my mind, that's all. Now," he glanced down at the notebook in his left hand, "you say she left at about ten o'clock?"

"Yes." Derek sighed. "She started to walk home, and I drove back home alone."

"How come she walked? The two of you have a fight?"

"No!" Then, calming down, Derek stared at the floor. "Just . . . well, just a disagreement, that's all."

"I see." The dark eyes bored into him again. "About what? The weather? Your relationship?" Derek didn't miss the sardonic tone of the sheriff's voice.

"No," Derek snapped back, flushing with embarrassment. "It was just . . . well . . ."

"Go on."

"She and my mom didn't get along too well. Mom's real religious, and she was upset about me dating someone who isn't. Wasn't. And Jenny—well, thought my mom was a fanatic."

"I see." The sheriff thought for a moment. "And you didn't try to follow her? To make up, maybe?"

"No. She said she didn't want to see me until I made up my mind who I wanted to be with. I figured I'd be

16

better off going home than trying to change her mind. She is—was—kind of stubborn." He felt a surge of loss welling up inside of him and wondered if he was going to break down, crying, in front of these two impassive spectators. Fighting back the tears, he tried to concentrate instead on the anger. Anger that Jenny was gone, anger that they seemed to think that he'd done it. "Aren't I supposed to have a lawyer or something?" he asked through clenched teeth.

"Only if you're arrested, son," the sheriff replied. "And we aren't arresting anyone. Yet." He paused significantly. "I'd rather keep this kind of informal at the moment. I'm sure you're going through enough strain as it is. We'll let you know if you need a lawyer, trust me."

Why should I trust you? Derek wondered. *You think I killed Jenny.* Aloud, he said: "It was her horoscope."

"Beg pardon?"

"Her horoscope," Derek explained. "She always read it. Yesterday it said she'd argue with a loved one, and she was sort of itching for a fight."

"So you did fight?" The dark eyes fastened on his face again.

Ooops. Wrong. Swallowing, Derek shook his head. "She was—well, looking for trouble. Really tense, you know? She really believes—believed—in that horoscope junk." He scowled. "Maybe you should talk to whoever writes those things for the school paper. It was their fault. They made her decide to get mad."

Sheriff Adkins simply raised an eyebrow. "Leave the suspicions to us, son," he said gently. "That's our line of work. You just answer my questions and we'll get along

17

fine. All I'm really looking for here is a good reason to take your name off my list of suspects."

Derek felt empty. Then, in his heart, he found himself getting angrier and angrier about this whole horoscope thing. If it hadn't been for Jenny's horoscope, she wouldn't have argued with his mother. She would still be alive. There was something about that stupid column that was clearly evil. . . .

Mr. Traynor was one of the youngest teachers on the staff at Fremont High. He dressed casually and had baby-faced good looks. At least a couple of the girls in Robyn's class had not-so-secret crushes on him. Robyn didn't—he was a Scorpio and not compatible with her sign. Besides, he was a teacher, and teacher-student relationships were a big no-no. And, to top it all off, he was intensely dry and boring.

He stared at Robyn from behind his desk, droning on and on about her poor grades and how he would be forced to fail her unless she picked them up—a lot. "And frankly, Robyn, I don't place much credence in that possibility," he told her. He was twiddling with a pencil as he talked, and she wished he would drop it or stick it up his nose or something. It was very distracting.

She cast a sidelong look at the other pupil in the room with her. Jeff Goldstein was almost her exact opposite: he was tall, wore tear-shaped glasses, and had a shock of dark hair that kept falling over his eyes when he nodded. He might have been sort of attractive in an odd way, except for two deadly flaws.

First of all, he was a science genius. He breezed through computer classes, scored perfectly on all math and science tests, and seemed to be in love with text-books. She couldn't recall ever seeing him outside of a classroom without a book in his hands. Science fiction, mostly, when he wasn't reading science fact. He probably read history books for something light. He took this whole education thing too strongly.

Secondly, he was a loner. He sometimes talked to a couple of other students, but never seemed to go out. Robyn had never seen him at the town's only movie theater, or at the mall. She knew he hated sports—a good thing, considering how bad he was at them. Over the years, he had drifted in and out of several of the school's crowds, but seemed happier alone. The only guy he seemed to get along with—oddly enough—was Alan MacKenzie, one of the biggest jocks in the school. Jeff had never been out on a date with any girl who would admit it. Robyn imagined him romancing a computer screen.

Mr. Traynor was finally winding down. Robyn tried to look as if she'd been listening to every word and nodded. "So," he said, "I've decided that there is only one way to raise your grade sufficiently to allow you to pass the course this year." He looked down at his notes. "Frankly, this is more for my sake than for yours. I don't think I could take it if you had to redo the year. One more flaky essay from you, and I'll scream. Anyway, I'm teaming you with Jeff here on the science fair project."

"What?" Both Robyn and Jeff cried out in unison, and Robyn saw that he was as shocked as she was. "But, Mr. Traynor!" she begged. *Not Jeff Goldstein!* she prayed. *Talk about fates worse than death!*

"But, sir," Jeff protested. "I could do much better

alone." He glanced at Robyn and turned a very bright shade of pink. "Uh, I don't mean to be rude, but—well, you suck at science."

"I'm glad to see I've made you both so happy," the teacher said, without a trace of a smile. "That's my decision, and you're stuck with it. Unless you'd like me to flunk you both here and now?"

Robyn looked at Jeff and shuddered. Then, reluctantly, she shook her head. "No, sir."

"Good." Mr. Traynor looked at Jeff. "And you, Jeff?"

"Why me, sir?" he asked, almost in tears.

"Because you're the only person in class who might still pass the course even with Miss Chantry's—ah—help."

Robyn was furious, but kept her temper in check. She was embarrassed that Jeff didn't want her with him, even though she didn't want him, either. How dare he? Finally, still bright pink, Jeff shrugged. "I guess I'll do it," he said.

"Fine." Mr. Traynor closed his notes. "Well, you two work out the details together. You can put in a summary of your project whenever you're ready. Dismissed."

Debi, Dana, and Natalie were waiting outside the door when Robyn came out. They looked at her and shook their heads when they saw her expression.

"Looks like you lost a battle," Dana said.

"Yeah," Debi agreed. "What happened? Did he flunk you?"

"Worse than that," Robyn said, wincing. "I got saddled with Jeff Goldstein as a partner in the science fair."

Natalie raised her eyebrows in surprise. "Hey, way to go! With him, you can't lose. Lucky thing."

"Well, I might be," Robyn admitted. "Except it means I'll have to see him in my spare time. Which I don't need. I'm tense enough about Jenny."

Debi grimaced, then gave her a wicked smile. "Well, you're not seeing anybody else, are you?" She had told Robyn over and over that she had been dumb to let Bryan Stockwell go. That was because she didn't know the details of the breakup, and Robyn had absolutely no intention of telling her. Considering what had happened, she doubted that Bryan would tell anyone how he'd really broken his wrist, either.

"Get real," Robyn said with a sigh. "Jeff Goldstein's about as attractive as—ow!" Debi suddenly kicked her on the ankle. Robyn glanced around and saw that Jeff was standing behind her, looking uncertain. "Oh. Er— hi, Jeff." She hoped he hadn't overheard her. If he had, her GPA just dropped a few more points.

He nodded, as if afraid to open his mouth. Shuffling from foot to foot, he finally said, "Look, I know you don't want to work with me, or anything. But we're stuck with it. So, how about meeting me in the computer room after school? I can show you a couple of ideas I've been working on for the science fair."

Robyn nodded to Jeff. "Sure. Good idea. I'll see you then."

Jeff nodded, then retreated fast down the corridor.

Natalie and Dana collapsed onto each other, laughing. "Whoo!" Natalie giggled. "Looks like you got yourself a new boyfriend!"

"Oh—*grow up*!" Robyn snapped.

"Why?" Dana asked. "Everybody knows he hasn't got any feelings. He's like a computer."

"Uh oh," Debi said, breaking up the argument. "Look who's coming."

Robyn glanced down the corridor and saw that Derek Vine was walking straight toward them. Rumors about him had been flying around school all day, but the police hadn't arrested him yet. Robyn didn't believe half of what had been said about him: before this, he'd been popular enough, and nobody had any real complaints about his behavior. Privately, she wasn't sure he'd either have the courage or the drive to kill anyone, let alone Jenny Warren.

He stopped and glared at them all. Robyn could see that he'd been crying. His eyes were puffed up and red. *He must miss her a lot*, she realized.

"I know that one of you four must be writing that dumb horoscope column for the school paper," he said coldly. He seemed to be searching for some sign of guilt in their eyes.

Actually, only the other three girls and the newspaper's teacher/adviser, Ms. Tepper, knew that Robyn was Jean Stephenson. It was no big deal, really, but when Robyn had announced she would be using a fake name for the column, Debi, Dana, and Natalie had laughed. As a joke, they had decided that *they* would use fake names for the columns and articles that they wrote, too. And that they'd keep who was who a secret. It had been kind of childish, really, but fun. Another way of keeping other students outside of the Gang of Four. The joke had died fairly early on, and the secret had been kept more out of habit than intent.

"Well," Derek continued, "whichever one of you it is can just think about this: if that dumb column hadn't said that Jenny would have a fight with a loved one last night, she'd have stayed with me and be alive right now. So it's the astrologer's fault she's dead." He looked at them and there was a depth of grief in his eyes Robyn had never seen in anyone before. "And when I find out which of you is writing that column," he added, "I'm going to make you wish *you* were dead."

Then, spinning on his heels, he strode off, not looking back.

Debi let her breath out in a sudden burst. "Phew!" she said. "He's really steamed." She looked at Robyn. "I hope you feel properly warned."

Robyn bit her lower lip nervously. "He didn't really mean that," she said uncertainly. "He's just grieving. It couldn't be my fault that Jenny's dead." *Could it?* She had never been exactly close to Jenny, but she had liked what she had seen of her. The idea that it might have been her fault that Jenny was dead was . . . impossible, she hoped.

Natalie looked at her and there was worry in her eyes. "I wouldn't take that threat too lightly," she advised her friend. "After all, the police think he's committed one murder already. Do you think he'd be bothered about killing someone else?"

Shaking, Robyn looked at her friends' faces. They all looked worried. But—she didn't have anything to be scared of—did she?

FOUR

AQUARIUS: School and family life could be better. A new relationship will change your point of view. Stay open-minded.

Jeff was furious with himself for being so flustered when he had talked to Robyn Chantry. He'd never been good at talking to girls, especially the pretty ones. And Robyn was certainly one of the best-looking girls in the school—her flame-red hair was hard to forget. And, like a real flame, it drew boys like moths to flitter around her. Jeff only wished he had the courage to be one of them. But his nerve had always failed him, not only with Robyn, but with every other girl he wanted to date.

And now, here he was, an opportunity to get to know her better handed to him on a plate. So what did he do? Blew the first conversation with her because of his own stupidity and the taunting of her stupid friends. Natalie and Dana were really shallow, and he knew he shouldn't let their giggling and comments get to him, but he couldn't help it.

It was typical that Robyn would have friends like that. She was such a ditz, useless in classes that mattered. She probably had the IQ of a hard-boiled egg. Not his type. But she *was* unforgettably pretty. And she had broken up with Bryan Stockwell. . . . Jeff shuddered, trying to bring himself back to reality. She wouldn't be interested in him in a million years. And besides, he'd overheard Bry telling the other jocks how he'd scored with Robyn. Jeff wasn't sure he actually believed Bryan's tales of conquest and passion—they sounded like lines from *Playboy* or something. But if Robyn was that kind of girl, did he really want to get to know her better?

He fought down the obvious answer to that.

"Hey, slow down!"

Wrenched out of his introspection, Jeff looked up and saw Alan MacKenzie heading across to him. Alan was one of the few people in his classes that he was friends with, despite their many differences. Alan was good with computers—which had brought them together in the first place—but he was also fairly athletic. He had always been on the track team, but his one big aim in school was to make the basketball team. Jeff knew the trials were being held after school today. Alan was casual and easygoing, and had a steady girl, Tashira Kent, who took up most of his spare time. He'd tried to get Jeff to double-date with him, but Jeff had always managed to get out of it. He didn't dare ask a girl out himself, and he was reluctant to let Alan pick one for him. Not because Alan was black, but because he had different tastes. Jeff didn't care one way or the other about the color of either his friends or any prospective dates. In fact, he'd nursed a very serious crush on Carolyn Hill for several months until she'd started dating some other guy and squashed his fantasies. But Alan kept suggesting the weirdest people as perfect matches for Jeff, and Jeff was not *that* desperate.

Yet.

Alan's own choice of Tashira Kent as a steady was weird, for example. Alan was laid-back and on good terms with the whole world. Tashira was quiet, almost a wallflower, and intensely interested only in playing the cello—and dating Alan. She'd hardly spoken six words to Jeff, and he found her one of the dullest people he'd ever met. Still, Alan seemed very happy with her.

"You were in another world," Alan said, laughing. "Where's your head at?"

"Oh, I was just . . . thinking," Jeff told him. "Traynor had me in his office about the science fair. Get this. He's teamed me with Robyn Chantry."

Alan whistled. "Man, that's luck! She's a hot-looking number." He grinned. "Maybe you'll get lucky there. Although she *is* a bit on the flaky side, if you ask me." He made a circular motion with one finger by his temple. "Still, with the way she looks, who cares which dimension or past life her mind's inhabiting?"

Jeff shuffled uncomfortably. Alan's thoughts mirrored his own dreams a little too closely. "It's not going to be like that," he said. "It's strictly work."

"Only if you make it be," replied Alan. "She broke up with Bryan Stockwell, you know? She's available."

"Not for me," Jeff said miserably. "What could she possibly want from me?"

"You're too hard on yourself," his friend told him. "You're not that bad. 'Course, you're not as good as me, but who is?"

Jeff had to smile. "I'll think about it," he lied, knowing there was no way.

"Stop thinking and *act*," Alan advised him. "Your trouble is that you do too much thinking. You think yourself right out of all your chances. Take my advice— get to know her a bit, show her what a genius you are, then hit her for a date. I'll bet she says yes."

"And if she doesn't?"

"How much worse off could you be? You'd be back where you started from. Then you go after someone else."

Jeff winced. "And she'll tell her friends, and they'll die laughing."

"Oh—so that's it." Alan shook his head. "Look—if they laugh at you, it just goes to show how shallow they are, right?"

"I can't take it like that," Jeff admitted. "It hurts too much."

"Then get back at them. If you get Robyn to go out with you, they'll stop laughing."

"And if she says no, they'll laugh more." Jeff sighed. "I just can't chance it."

"Faint heart never won fair lady," Alan quoted to him. "Yours is the faintest heart I've ever seen. And— after Tashira, of course—Robyn Chantry is one of the fairest ladies."

Jeff wasn't convinced. He *wanted* to be, but he was too scared of the possible outcome. Changing the subject, he asked, "You all set for the trials tonight?"

27

"Ready and raring to go." Alan grinned. "I'm gonna dazzle them with magic!" He spun around and made a mock throw for the hoop.

Unfortunately, at that moment Derek Vine was trying to get past them. Alan's outflung arm gave Derek a glancing blow. There was silence for a second, then Derek went red with anger.

"You clumsy idiot," he said furiously. "Why don't you watch what you're doing?"

Alan put his hands up defensively. "Hey, I'm sorry! It was just an accident."

"It was stupidity," Derek snapped. "And I've had enough of that for one day."

"I said I was sorry," Alan told him. "Let's leave it at that, okay?"

Derek glared at him. "Fine. Just keep out of my way. The less I see of your black face, the better I'll like it."

Jeff knew that was definitely the wrong thing for Derek to have said, but it was too late now. Alan's eyes narrowed and his body tensed.

"You got a problem with my skin color?" he asked, dangerously gently. "Because if you have, the next time I hit you won't be accidental. And it won't be light."

Derek seemed to realize he'd gone too far. He looked up at Alan—who had a good six inches and about thirty pounds on him. He shook his head, slightly more subdued. "I don't give a damn what color your skin is," he snarled. "Just stay away from me." Then he turned and stormed away.

Putting a hand on Alan's arm, Jeff could feel the tension in his friend's muscles. "Let it go," he advised.

"Derek's had a bad day. You heard about his girlfriend getting murdered?"

Alan took a deep breath, then let it out slowly and nodded. "Yeah. Yeah, I heard about that." He blinked and looked down at Jeff. "You're right, he's just hurting inside. He probably didn't mean anything by it." Then he looked off down the corridor. "But he'd better not say anything like that again. Unless he wants to see the inside of a hospital."

After classes were over, Jeff headed down to the computer room, his stomach churning. He'd run through the upcoming meeting with Robyn a hundred times in his head. Sometimes his fantasies had her swooning into his arms. Others had her laughing in his face. What scared him was that he didn't know which he'd find easier to deal with. Anyway, nothing would happen between them. She'd most likely act like he wasn't even alive.

The room was empty when he arrived. Slinging down his bag, he took out the diskette he'd put his ideas onto and booted it up. Which one of the possibilities would she be most likely to go for?

"Hi," Robyn said, coming into the room. Jeff looked up and found himself blushing again. She really was pretty. And she seemed so cool, so self-assured. Robyn tossed her bag onto the desk nearest to him, then pulled over a chair to join him. "So, what's this?"

He found her physical presence more distracting than he'd imagined. Her left knee was quite close to his, and she was leaning over to look at the screen. He caught a whiff of some faint perfume. Swallowing hard, he managed to say, "My menu of what I've been working on for the science fair."

She nodded, reading the list. Then she made a face. "God, it's so boring! Chess, finance master, census projection—don't you ever lighten up? I was hoping we could do something halfway fun."

Well, yeah, he had one or two ideas, but they didn't involve a computer. He shook his head, embarrassed that she thought his ideas were so dull. "I—I just figured on doing something in a new sort of way." He managed to look at her. "Of course, I'm always open to suggestions."

"I don't know much about computers," she told him, "or I wouldn't be here now. I'd be doing something more interesting."

Terrific—she'd admitted she didn't want to be with him. It was what he'd feared. Trying to hide the hurt and disappointment, he said, "Well, what would you find more interesting? Super Mario Brothers?"

"Don't get sarcastic with me," she said coolly.

"No," he said, flustered. "I didn't mean that was all you could do. I meant—well, what would you find interesting?"

Robyn gave him a look, then turned her attention back to the screen. "It's all so—impersonal," she objected. "Money, statistics, logic . . . they all seem so dry." She sighed. "My horoscope told me it was going to be a bad day."

"Oh, great," he muttered, unable to stop his big mouth. "I'm stuck with Shirley MacLaine for the science fair."

"What do you know about it?" Robyn asked,

frowning. "Just because you don't believe in something doesn't mean you should make fun of it."

"Come on!" he said. "Horoscopes are for weak-minded people who are too scared to make decisions on their own. They need the approval of the stars!"

"For your information," she said, clearly controlling her temper, "astrology is the oldest science known to man. Many prominent people believe in it. And the stars simply guide us—they don't rule our lives."

"Astrology a science?" Jeff said, unable to keep the sneer out of his voice. "Why not go back to reading the entrails of chickens?"

"I knew this was a mistake," Robyn said, her face almost as red as her hair. "I don't need this." She reached for her bag.

Surprised at himself, Jeff grabbed her hand. "You *do* need this," he told her. "We both do, or we flunk out. Look, I'm sorry I made fun of astrology. It's just—well, I believe in the real world, not fairy-tale mumbo jumbo."

Robyn took a breath and nodded. "Okay, you're right," she said. "I'm sorry if I blew up. But astrology really is a science."

"Prove it," he challenged her.

"What?"

"Prove it," Jeff repeated. "If it's a science, then it's possible to prove it. Show me how the stars can possibly have any effect on us."

Robyn frowned. "You're serious?"

"Yes." He gestured at the computer. "That's what I call science. You do math on it, and you get the same answer every time. But you can give two astrologers the

31

same information and they come up with wildly different answers."

"That's because numbers aren't people," Robyn replied. "They don't have any choice in what they do. Two and two always equals four because numbers don't have a will of their own. If they did, maybe they'd want to equal five once in a while, just for a change."

He laughed, but with her. She smiled and carried on.

"The stars influence us because we're starstuff ourselves. Since you like science so much, tell me—where did all of the atoms that make up the earth and everything on it come from?"

Astronomy was one of his favorite subjects. "Supernovas," he told her. "Originally, all the matter in the universe was hydrogen. Stars use that to glow, and they join the hydrogen atoms together. This releases energy and makes more complicated atoms. Then, eventually, the star will run out of hydrogen and explode. This scatters those atoms throughout space. Some of them eventually became planets, like the earth."

"Right," she said triumphantly. "Every single atom in our bodies was once inside a star. We're made from the stars. Of course they influence us. It makes sense."

"That's poetry, not proof," he told her.

"Just because it's poetic doesn't make it wrong."

"Well, okay."

Robyn smiled again. Jeff liked the effect it had on her face—and his emotions. "I'll bet you're an Aquarius, right?" she asked.

"Yeah," he agreed, surprised. "How did you know?"

"You have all the earmarks of one—demanding logic

and proof, but open to being convinced. Aquarians are good at both poetry and electronics."

He laughed uncertainly. "But one-twelfth of the population aren't poetic electricians," he pointed out.

"That's because the stars don't rule us," Robyn told him. "They simply influence us. We have to make our own lives and decisions, but it helps to know what's going on." She thought for a moment. "It's like making the best use of all of the information that you can get. To me, that makes sense."

"All right," he conceded. Assume for now that she might just be right. Which meant . . . "It gives me an idea for a project."

"What?"

"Why don't we try to prove that horoscopes work? Match predictions to accuracy by computer? We could write a program that will work out the chances of horoscopes coming true by accident or by design. If astrology really is a science, that should be possible." And it would combine her interest with his. Maybe win her over onto his side a bit.

Robyn shook her head. "Astrology isn't something mechanical," she told him. "It's as much to do with intuition and feeling as with facts. And you can't program those into a computer. That's a really stupid idea. Find something else."

Jeff sighed. She demanded that he create their project, then shot down his suggestions. He could see that this relationship was going to be even harder than he'd guessed.

FIVE

TAURUS: Some highs, but a very bad day overall. Watch out for arguments and avoid following bad advice.

He waited in the shadows once again. In the week since he'd taken Jenny Warren's sacrifice, he had been watching and waiting for the right moment to make his next move. Now was the time—the stars had spoken.

Life was a vast wheel, turning slowly behind the superficial mask that was shown the world. But he had seen the reality. He knew that the wheel of life and death was the wheel of the Zodiac. The stars had spoken to mankind, laid down their unbreakable laws. Most people had ignored it, but not him. He had heard the song, the music of the spheres, and he was an embodiment of the truth. He was one in purpose with the stars. He was their messenger.

Tonight, the message was death.

He fingered his star-selected weapon and smiled to

himself. Tonight the second stage in the great wheel would be filled. In just a very short while.

Alan was feeling high. Making the team last week had been his greatest wish fulfilled, and he had been practicing hard ever since. He was good and he knew it. Basketball was his life—that, and Tashira, of course. He'd shot some great hoops in practice, and felt really good about the world.

His horoscope in the school newspaper had said it would be a bad day, but it was certainly wrong this time. Except there had been another run-in with Derek Vine. It had been Derek's place that Alan had taken on the team—Derek had been pushed back to second string. Several times during practice Derek had tried to make him look bad. None of them had worked, and eventually Derek had been caught by the coach as he was trying to foul Alan. That had earned him a verbal lashing, and Derek had promised to get Alan back before storming off.

Still, though that was unpleasant, it hadn't ruined Alan's day. Derek had lost his first-string place on the team, after all. He knew that Derek was under a lot of pressure—it was only a week since Jenny Warren had been murdered, and she'd been buried only the day before. It was bound to mess Derek up. The fact that the police kept talking to Derek was making him more and more nervous.

Alan himself didn't think that Derek was guilty of the deed. True, he had a bad temper at times, but that didn't make him a murderer. It was also true that he was kind of opinionated and ruled by his mother's beliefs. But he wasn't a bad person at heart, and Alan could tell that Derek was at least trying to correct his personality problems.

Oh well. None of that mattered. Alan walked through the night, heading for Tashira's house. This was the night for some cool music and hot love!

The watcher smiled to himself as he saw the victim walking down the road. Alan MacKenzie looked happy, which was only right: he must know that his destiny was about to be fulfilled. In a few moments, he would again be one with the stars in the vast circle of life and death.

His would be the house of death.

The watcher found himself getting excited. To be the representative of the Zodiac was a great honor. But he had to be careful—too much enjoyment of his work might make him clumsy. *Calm down, be prepared . . .* He looked down at the knife, just to be certain it was ready. He liked this knife—when he had first seen it, he had known that it was the perfect tool for this situation. The hilt fitted smoothly in his hand, and the twin blades of the knife were fascinating. Like the two horns of a bull. He'd practiced with it until he was certain that he wouldn't make any mistakes.

The sacrifice was almost upon him. Eager, the watcher stepped forward in the shadows, and stepped on a stick.

The sound in the evening silence was like a rifle shot. Alan looked around.

"Who's there?" he called. Suspicious, but not apprehensive. That was okay.

The watcher stepped out of the shadows, the knife hidden behind his back. "Hello, Alan," he said softly.

Alan relaxed his tensed muscles. "Oh, it's you. Boy, you sure gave me a fright." He grinned. He was close enough now. . . .

The grin died as Alan saw the knife. Before he had a chance to speak, the watcher stabbed him—a perfect blow. The blades lashed into the young man's chest. With a choking gasp, Alan fell forward to the ground. The impact drove the knife even deeper into his chest.

Nodding to himself, the watcher bent and turned Alan's body over. There seemed to be blood everywhere —it was amazing how much a human body held. Luckily, he was wearing gloves, and none of it got onto his clothing. He admired the workmanship of the knife, and the artistry of the angle he'd struck. Then he checked for a pulse. There was none.

The sacrifice had been perfect.

He looked at the body and was happy to see that it didn't need any work at all. The shock on Alan's face, the knife—it was just right. Taking his camera out, he took a flash picture of the body, and then a second, to be absolutely certain.

"Thank you, Alan," he told the corpse. "You've been a great help. Rest in peace, my friend." Then, whistling happily to himself, he walked off into the night.

SIX

LEO: Bad news early on is compounded by the attitudes of others. Try to be flexible, and work on relationships.

Robyn bolted her breakfast quickly to give herself time to check on her father's progress before school. After throwing the dishes into the sink, she ran to her father's workshop.

She tapped on the door and went in. As always, he was hard at work. A fresh batch of candles was on the lowest shelf and he was examining them for flaws. He put down the human-faced tree he was checking and smiled at her.

"Morning, sweetie," he called. "How's it going?"

She came over and kissed his cheek. "Oh, pretty good. I wanted to see how your special projects were coming before I go to school."

He laughed. "Impatient! They'll be done soon enough."

"Oh, come on," she begged. "Just a little look . . ."

Shaking his head, he got up and went to his cupboard. "All right." He took out the first of the chess pieces he had made and showed it to her. It was the black queen, cast entirely in black wax. She was tall, imperious, and had a long, regal face. In her right hand she carried a scepter, and in the top of the wand was a small zirconium. "The sorceress queen," he explained. "Queen of the night, if you like. It's the first of the chess set I'm making for John and Fern. You like it?"

"It's beautiful," Robyn said sincerely. "You're in top form, Dad."

"We try to please." He laughed, replacing the piece and closing the cupboard. "Now, off to school before your mother gets impatient."

"What about that Vlad the Impaler sculpture?" she asked him.

He shrugged. "I'm still doing research on it. There's no hurry, though."

Robyn read behind the words. "You're putting it off," she accused him.

He rubbed his temples. "I guess I am," he admitted. "I really don't like glorifying violence. It's giving me headaches just planning that piece."

There was the sound of the horn from outside. Robyn smiled. "That's Mom, threatening to go without me again." She gave her father another kiss. "Just forget about the Vlad piece and concentrate on the chess set. That's fantastic work. Bye!"

Her mother had the van in motion as soon as Robyn was in it and had fastened her seat belt. Pulling out into the road, her mom asked, "So, how's the science project going?"

"Not too well," Robyn admitted. "Jeff Goldstein's such—oh, I don't know. One minute he seems like a regular guy, the next he's ranting about science being the key to understanding, and what a crock my beliefs are."

"It takes all kinds to make a world," Mrs. Chantry said. "Though there are some I'd cheerfully do without. Like Mrs. Vine."

"Oh." Robyn sighed. Derek's mother. "What's she done now?"

"Not much. She was in the shop again yesterday handing out tracts and annoying the customers. I had to get Ray to throw her out. I don't begrudge her her beliefs, but I wish she'd show the same consideration to other people."

"She's like her son," Robyn said, wincing as they almost sideswiped a Ford. "He's very opinionated, too."

Her mother smiled. "And you're not?"

"Well, at least I'm open-minded, and don't thrust my beliefs down people's throats."

"A minute ago it sounded to me as though this Jeff Goldberg thinks you are."

"Goldstein," Robyn corrected. "And he *asked* me to try and convince him. Then he complained about it. I just don't understand the guy. Sometimes he almost spooks me. He keeps *looking* at me."

Her mother laughed. "You're a very pretty girl, Robyn. I'd be worried about him if he didn't look."

"Yes, but it's not like he wants to ask me out or anything. He just looks."

"Perhaps he's just too shy. Why don't you ask him?"

Robyn made a face. "He's not my type." She thought he was nice enough, but there was something kind of weird about him. Like he was hiding something.

"I hope you're not still moping about that Stockwell boy," her mother said, a trifle sharply. "Put him behind you."

"I'm not moping about him. Honest."

Mrs. Chantry sniffed. "If you'd have listened to the cards, dear, you could have avoided all of that. I *told* you from the start what he was like."

Robyn didn't answer. It was true. Her mother had never liked Bryan, and she had been right. But did she have to keep bringing it up?

They had reached the Smolinske house, and Mrs. Chantry pulled into the driveway. Debi came out, carrying her usual packed bag, and slid into the rear seat. Mrs. Chantry smiled and started to back out. "Your father's car still not fixed?" she asked, a wicked gleam in her eye.

"Broken again," Debi said with a sigh. "And back in the shop. I figure the garage owner must know it better than we do by now."

"That's the trouble with shopping by appearances," Mrs. Chantry remarked. "No depth." She looked pointedly at her daughter. "The same thing applies to boys, you know. Go for staying power, not good looks."

"I'm not going for either," Robyn replied. "At the moment, I'm just sticking to schoolwork."

"Right!" Debi said. "You're training to become a nun! Natalie reckons that Jeff Goldstein's got his eye on you."

Robyn felt herself going red. "Natalie's just looking

41

for gossip. There are days when I don't particularly like her, you know."

"Then don't hang around with her, dear," Mrs. Chantry advised. "A person is known by the company they keep."

"Honestly, Mom," Robyn said. "I don't know where you get all these corny sayings from."

"I have a salesman who comes to the shop. I get a discount on them."

"I believe it."

Mrs. Chantry dropped them at the school, then drove off to open the store. Debi grinned. "Your mother is pretty neat."

"She's okay," Robyn agreed. "I guess I'll keep her." Together they walked into the main building and headed for their lockers. Natalie and Dana were there, along with the school custodian, Joe Butler. He was working on Natalie's locker.

"What's happening?" Debi asked. Natalie rolled her eyes.

"Just some stuff fallen against the lock," Joe said. He gave her a smile and carried on working. "Have it fixed in a minute. You shouldn't put so much stuff in here," he told Natalie.

"You should keep your opinions to yourself," she answered rudely. "I'm not interested in them."

Joe stopped working and looked at her. He was in his early forties, with a touch of gray at his temples. Still, he was pretty muscular, and aside from the limp in his right leg, in very good shape. The only thing marring his looks was a slight scar down the right side of his face. He'd gotten his injuries from a terrorist bomb while he was in the Army, serving in Germany. Invalided out, he'd returned to his hometown and taken the custodian job in the school. He was quite popular, and Robyn liked him.

"I know I'm just the janitor," he said to Natalie. "But I still deserve a little politeness. Especially when I'm helping you out."

Natalie looked like she was going to say something snappish, but then looked down. "I'm sorry."

"Apology accepted." He bent back to work on the locker.

Robyn looked up and saw Derek Vine approaching them. He'd been in a pretty lousy mood for the past week, since Jenny had been killed. He still seemed to blame her death on her horoscope in the paper, but he still didn't know who "Jean Stephenson" really was. He had been constantly needling the four girls, trying to get a rise out of one of them. The others had backed Robyn up, and hadn't told him it was her. Robyn couldn't help feeling sorry for him, even though he obviously didn't appreciate her concern. "How's it going?" she asked gently.

He looked at her, and there was only hurt and anger in his eyes. "I haven't forgotten about this horoscope business," he said coldly. "I know one of you is to blame for Jenny's death. And whoever it is is going to regret it. This junk about the stars is evil."

Joe looked up. "Don't be so closed-minded. I believe in it myself. I even read Jean Stephenson's column in the school paper. She's really good, you know." He smiled, and Robyn couldn't tell if he was serious or not.

"It was because of that column that Jenny got killed," Derek said angrily. "And I'm going to set things right."

"You can't blame a horoscope for killing somebody," Robyn said, not for the first time. "It's just a general prediction."

"The Bible says that astrology is evil," Derek replied. "And I agree." He gave them one last glare and walked off.

Natalie laughed. "I'm sure God must be very happy to hear that Derek Vine has approved of the Bible."

"Knock it off, Natalie," Debi said. "He's still upset about Jenny. It must be really hard to lose someone you love. He'll come back down to earth again soon." She looked at her friend. "What's gotten into you lately? You're so edgy and snappy."

"It's—" Natalie started to say, but she was interrupted.

"Uh oh." Robyn pointed down the corridor. "Look who's there."

The others followed her finger, and saw Sheriff Adkins entering the building. He headed for the principal's office.

"I wonder what's going on?" Dana said.

Joe looked up, and the locker door sprang open. A pile of magazines flopped out. "Finished," he said. "That's what jammed the lock. They must have fallen against it on the inside." Then he looked down the corridor at the sheriff's retreating back. "Didn't you guys hear? There was another murder last night." When four shocked faces looked up at him, he added, "Young Alan MacKenzie was stabbed to death."

"Oh, God!" Debi breathed. "Do they—do they know who did it?"

"I don't think so," replied Joe. "But the sheriff seems to have something in mind."

Robyn felt almost giddy with shock. She leaned against the wall and took deep breaths. Two murders in a week! And Alan MacKenzie . . . She stiffened in shock. He was Jeff's best friend! Had Jeff heard the news yet? How was he taking it?

She found out later. When she went to the computer room after school to work on their science fair project, Jeff was there ahead of her, staring blankly out of the window. She had to say his name twice before he realized she was there and turned around.

He'd obviously been crying, but tried to cover it up. Alan's murder must have hit him pretty hard. "We can put this off, if you like," Robyn said gently. "I heard about Alan. I'm really sorry." She didn't know what else to say. Most guys didn't like to have attention drawn to the fact that they'd been crying. But she couldn't just ignore it, could she? She wished for a moment that she knew him better, knew what might comfort him.

"No," he answered, shaking his head. "I need something to take my mind off . . . Look, let's try to decide on a topic today, okay?"

Robyn nodded and went to join him at the window. "Any ideas yet?" she asked.

"I don't know." Jeff looked at her, and she saw that he was trying, but that the news was affecting him a lot. "Since you're so much into this horoscope nonsense, I still think that might be something to look at."

"But I told you—it's too personal. You can't get a computer to interpret people's behavior."

"You don't have to," Jeff said. "Look, a computer is just a tool. Like a pencil, or a paintbrush, or a screwdriver. It does some things really well. Routine stuff, calculations, that sort of thing."

"So?"

"Well, I was thinking about your casting horoscopes. I know you do some sort of calculations. I've seen you scribbling away."

"You've been watching me," she accused him, but without anger.

"I can't help it," he told her. "Your red hair makes you stand out."

Robyn realized that Jeff was so distracted by Alan's death that he didn't seem to be censoring his thoughts and feelings anymore. She stared at him, and he mistook her gaze.

"I'm sorry. I shouldn't have said that." He started to blush and looked down at the floor. "I didn't really mean it the way it sounded."

For the first time, Robyn wondered if Jeff was interested in her. And if he was, how would she feel about it? No, the whole idea was ludicrous. "That's all right," she told him. "I guess it does." She waited for him to follow up, but he seemed to have lost his courage again. He was a very changeable person. Or a very uncertain one.

"Anyway, I had this idea," he told her. "If you tell me exactly how you calculate your horoscopes, maybe we can work out a way for the computer to help a bit."

Robyn nodded and sat down, applying herself to their project. "Okay, let's try it from the ground up." She rooted in her bag for her pad and the copy of *Raphael's Ephemeris*. "When were you born?"

"1975," he told her.

"What a coincidence," she said dryly. "So was I. Can you be a bit more specific?"

"Oh, yeah. February first."

"Aquarius, right. Do you know what time of day?"

Jeff thought for a moment. "About three in the afternoon. Is it important?"

"Yes." She noted this down. "Okay, what we do is use this information to find out what the sky looked like when you were born. Then we can work out the influences on you."

He frowned. "I don't get it. You already know I'm Aquarius. What difference does the rest of it make?"

"Because each person's horoscope is unique—you have to calculate the positions of all of the planets, the ascendant—that's the zodiacal sign on the horizon when you were born—and things like that."

He pointed to the *Ephemeris*. "And that helps?"

"Yes. It's a listing of where all of the planets were in the night sky for the last century or so, and where they will be, so I can predict what the future might hold. But I have to make corrections, of course."

"Why?"

"Because it's all in Greenwich Mean Time, not local time. We have to correct for that. Then we have to correct for the fact that our little town of Fremont, Wisconsin, is ninety degrees west of Greenwich, which means that the sky will be slightly different over here than it would say in the charts. You were born here, weren't you?"

Jeff nodded.

"Then, finally, we look up where the planets were on any given day."

Jeff started laughing. Thinking he was making fun of her again, she snapped, "If you aren't going to treat me seriously—"

Jeff stopped and looked a little embarrassed. "It's not that," he told her. "It's just strange. You think math is dull and useless—but you're completely comfortable working out this complicated equation. To be honest, if you can do what you said, you'll find computer programming a snap."

Robyn realized that he was complimenting her. "Thank you." It felt good to have his approval, though his opinion didn't really matter.

"Although, of course," he added, "it all seems a bit pointless." Before she could say anything, he held up his hand. "I'm not attacking your beliefs—just your methods. Look, this is exactly what a computer could do for you. Wouldn't it save you a lot of time and energy if a computer could calculate the sky chart for you?"

"I suppose so," Robyn agreed thoughtfully.

"Then why not make that our science fair project?" Jeff suggested. "Use the computer not to *generate* the horoscopes, but to do all the tedious calculations. Instead of having to look up your information and make corrections, we can create a program that would do that for you—if you type in the date, time of birth, and the place. It would take the computer a couple of seconds at most. Instead of half an hour or so for you."

Robyn found herself warming up to Jeff. He really wasn't such a bad person. This idea did intrigue her—

she *hated* all of the calculations she had to do! "Okay," she agreed. "Let's give it a shot. Maybe old Twinkletoes did us both a favor after all."

"Yeah." Jeff gave her a glance, then looked quickly away. "I've got no complaints."

"Okay," Robyn said briskly. "Let's get to work." Robyn had once heard that a sure way to cure grief was to concentrate on something else. Maybe by working a lot on their science fair project, she could help Jeff get over his pain about Alan's death.

SEVEN

*SCORPIO: News is not good for you. People in authority
will be aggressive. Don't blame others for your own
failures.*

Derek's stomach was turning over as he looked up
once again at Sheriff Adkins. It was like a nightmare—
back in the same room, with that same silent deputy at
the door, and the sheriff asking sharp, barbed questions
while pretending that this was all a friendly chat.

Would this never end?

"Why are you picking on me?" he asked, scared.

"Son," the sheriff replied in a gentle voice, hitching
his trousers a little higher over his bulging stomach, "if
you think this is me being picky, you should hope you
never see me being downright mean."

"I haven't done anything," Derek said.

"Then you haven't got anything to worry about." The
sheriff looked down at his notes. "Whatever you may

think, I don't enjoy doing this to you. But it's my job, and I try to do my job as well as I can. I'm sure you can understand that. Now, once more. Where were you last night, about nine?"

"I was home. Listening to music. You want to know which albums and tracks?"

"There's no need to get smart, son. I'll tell you what I want you to tell me. If I wasn't such a patient soul, you'd be getting on my nerves by now. But I'm making allowances, understand? Now, can anybody back up your story? Your mother, maybe?"

Derek shook his head. "She was at a bible study class. She got home about ten fifteen."

"And you never left the house?"

"No."

Nodding, Sheriff Adkins made another entry in his book. "What did you and Alan MacKenzie argue about?"

Derek shifted uncomfortably. "When?"

"So you argued more than once?"

Great! That really put his foot in it! "We didn't get along real well," he finally admitted. "He rubbed me the wrong way, that's all."

"That's not all." The piercing eyes bored into him. "He took your place as starting guard on the basketball team, I hear. Now you're just the first reserve and need someone to drop out. Like MacKenzie did last night. Kind of permanently."

"I didn't do it!"

"I never said you did," the sheriff replied. "Just that you had a reason, maybe, to do it. He'd taken your place, and you didn't like that. You tried to foul him a few times last night at practice."

Squirming uncomfortably, Derek said: "I was mad, yeah." He looked up at his tormentor. "Look, my girlfriend was *murdered* a week ago. You thought I did that one, too."

"Not quite," corrected the sheriff.

"Maybe not in so many words," Derek yelled. "But you said it. And I can't get over it that easily. So I've been a little short-tempered lately. So sue me. Don't you think it's understandable?"

"Yes, son, I do," the sheriff replied, which surprised Derek. "Provided you didn't kill her," he added. " 'Cause if you *did* kill her, then I'd attribute your temper tantrums as fear of being caught." He spread his hands. "You see my problem? If you're innocent, your story makes sense. If you're guilty, the other story makes sense. Both fit the facts. It's just a matter of discovering which of them fits *all* of the facts. Until I do, I've got to treat both as equally likely. Now, after the practice in which you fouled MacKenzie, you went straight home to listen to music?"

Derek sighed. "Right. I wanted to calm down. Look, I lost my temper. I don't like it, but it happens. I try to control it. Listening to music cools me off."

"Hmm." Sheriff Adkins paused, chewing the end of his pencil thoughtfully. "You gotta admit, son, that it is kind of odd, when you think about it. You argue with Jenny Warren, and she's killed right afterward. Then you have a fight with Alan MacKenzie, and *he's* murdered." He stared down at Derek. "Stabbed by a double-bladed knife. Looks like he was gored to death by a bull. Not a pretty sight."

"I didn't do it," Derek said, scared.

"No?" The sheriff smiled. "Glad to hear it, son. Now all we have to do is to prove it. At this moment, we don't have any other suspects that look as likely as you." He paused. "Unless you think their horoscopes did them in."

"What?" Derek hadn't followed him.

"If you recall, you said it was her horoscope's fault that Jenny was murdered. That that day's prediction had been real bad. Well, I checked the school paper while I was waiting for you—and MacKenzie had a similarly bad reading for yesterday. Kind of a coincidence, don't you think?"

Derek felt a surge of hope—very like panic. "Well, maybe there *is* a link there?" he said wildly. "Maybe whoever writes that column is doing the killings. And that's her warning."

The sheriff snorted. "Kinda farfetched, isn't it?" he asked. "Killers don't usually warn their victims. Still . . . I wouldn't be doing my elected duty if I didn't check it out, I suppose." He picked up the copy of the school paper he'd been reading earlier and looked at the right page. "Jean Stephenson?" he said. "I don't recognize that student's name."

"It's an alias," Derek told him, his mind working feverishly. "Just like crooks use. No one will say who it really is. But it's got to be either Natalie Byrnes, Dana Mullalley, Robyn Chantry, or Debi Smolinske. It's always one of them who hands in the column, and they always hang out together. They're all a little flaky."

Making note of something, Sheriff Adkins nodded. "Well, I guess that's about all for now," he said. "You can go. I really hope you're telling me the truth, 'cause you seem like a nice enough kid. But I'm going to tell you—I got my eyes on you. If I think there's the slightest cause, I'll haul you in to jail so fast your head'll spin. If you're really innocent, then you should be reassured. But if you're guilty, you'd better be quaking in your boots, hear?"

Derek swallowed hard and nodded. He left the room meekly. Once outside, though, his expression changed to anger, and he slammed his fist hard against the wall. He didn't even notice the pain, or the streaks of blood he left behind.

Someone was going to pay for this. . . .

Jeff was really enjoying himself. He was scribbling down ideas on a notepad as he quizzed Robyn carefully about the exact way she worked out her horoscopes. She had decided that the easiest way to demonstrate was to work out his own reading, and had led him through it, step by step.

"So," she finished, "at three P.M. on February first, nineteen seventy-five, we have the following situation. The sun and Mercury were in Aquarius—hardly surprising. Venus and Jupiter were in Pisces. Saturn was in Cancer, the moon in Libra, and Mars in Capricorn."

"And what about Uranus, Neptune, and Pluto?" Jeff asked. "Don't they count?"

"Some astrologers think so, others don't. They're so far away from us that they don't change positions much, and so don't vary greatly in their effects."

"Okay." Jeff studied the circular chart Robyn had drawn up, with the symbols for the planets and constellations. "Now you know all of that, what does it mean?"

Robyn smiled. "Starting to believe me a little?"

"Not yet—but I'm always open to proof."

"I know," she replied. "That's from Mercury being in Aquarius. You're an observer who will take note of everything and then use it—even if it means changing your perceptions of reality."

He shrugged. "You're just guessing that because you know me."

"It's not guesswork," Robyn said. "It's all verifiable. Now—Venus is in Pisces. That's your emotional side. It means you have some kind of an artistic streak—maybe not art as such. Could be poetry, or something else creative. It also means that you tend to hide your feelings, keeping them to yourself. This can be a problem. It could make you miss out on things. Unless you learn to let your feelings show, you could not experience romance, for example." She looked at him thoughtfully. He went red and looked quickly away.

Did she know what he was thinking? he wondered, unable to stop his dumb reaction. *Was she dropping some kind of hint? Or was this just a business thing for her? If only he knew!*

"Jupiter in Pisces," Robyn continued after a moment, "means you're sensitive and compassionate. But it also means that you can be taken advantage of by people you trust or believe in. There's a tendency for you to look for security or illumination in religion, or some other system of belief. If you're convinced of the truth of some-

55

thing, you could become fanatical in pursuit of your goals.

"Saturn in Cancer—that signals repression, isolation. Often an unhappy childhood, too. Couple that with Venus, and you're really inclined to keep to yourself and hide what you feel, even from yourself if you can. The moon in Libra—you're willing to listen to advice, and you can be polite and charming when you set your mind to it. You hate show-offs and prefer to be low-key about things. You might even appear to be cold and aloof, but that's not your true nature. Finally, Mars in Capricorn. You've got a head for material success. You're thorough, efficient, and you really like to see a job through to its conclusion, neatly wrapped up. You could do very well in business."

Jeff looked at her uncertainly. A lot of what she'd said might have been from watching him—if she'd even bother doing that. But some of it was very close to the facts. Surprisingly close in places . . . Maybe there was something to this, after all?

How much of his thoughts she could guess, he didn't know. Robyn started to say something, but there was a rap on the door. They looked up, startled. Sheriff Adkins walked in.

"Not interrupting anything, am I?" he asked. He was carrying a copy of the school paper in his hand.

"Nothing much," Robyn replied, pulling slightly back from Jeff. "Is something wrong?"

"Just a few questions. I'm looking into the murder of Alan MacKenzie."

Alan's death! Jeff had completely forgotten about it

56

for a few minutes, being so absorbed with Robyn. He felt a pang of guilt and a deeper hurt from the loss.

"It was horrible," Robyn said, paling herself. "You want to speak to Jeff?"

"No, actually, I was looking for you," the sheriff told her.

"Me? But I hardly knew him."

Unfolding the paper, Sheriff Adkins held it out and tapped the horoscopes. "I talked to Miz Tepper. I understand you write this column?"

She frowned, puzzled. "Yes."

"Your entry for yesterday on Taurus—the victim's sign—warned about having a bad day. Now, in and of itself that isn't interesting. But the entry for Aries last week—when Jenny Warren was killed—also warned of a particularly bad day. That's sort of curious, wouldn't you say?"

Robyn looked stunned. "But—but there are lots of days that I say are bad for people, and nobody is killed!"

"Maybe so," the sheriff agreed lazily. "But how come this column is written by a nonexistent Jean Stephenson? Don't you want to get the credit for it? Or the blame?"

Robyn's face went almost as red as her hair. "I just thought that name sounded more astrological than my own. Like Jeanne Dixon, you know? I don't hide behind it."

"It's just that people don't know about it," the sheriff said. "Like Derek Vine."

"So that's it!" said Robyn angrily. "He's the one who started this. He still thinks I'm responsible for Jenny Warren being murdered!"

The sheriff's eyes were mere slits. "You haven't said why he doesn't know you write the column. He gave me four possible names. I talked to Miz Tepper, and she told me that it was you."

"It was just a game," Robyn explained. "Debi, Natalie, Dana, and I were just having some fun. We all created made-up people for our columns, and then wouldn't tell anyone who was who. We didn't mean anything by it." It sounded pretty silly, even to Jeff, and he could empathize with her horribly embarrassed expression.

"Maybe. Maybe not."

Jeff felt impatient. "Look, Sheriff," he said quietly. "Is this leading up to something? Just because Robyn writes horoscopes is no reason to grill her, surely?"

Sheriff Adkins turned to stare at him. "Look, son," he said gently, "I sympathize with your feelings. And with those of your girlfriend. But I've got a job to do, and that sometimes means following up on even silly-looking theories. So bear with me, okay?"

Jeff wanted to correct his mistaken impression that Robyn was his girlfriend, but he didn't get a chance. Robyn was irritated, and said, "So you think I had something to do with the killings, too?"

"Well, you did seem to predict them," the sheriff said. He reached into his pocket and pulled out a small photo of a scarf. "This woollen scarf wouldn't happen to belong to you, would it?"

Robyn looked at it and shook her head. "No. It does look vaguely familiar, though." She stared at it again. "Is this what was used to—kill Jenny?"

"Uh huh." The sheriff took another picture out, then

58

hesitated. "Look, this one's kind of gruesome. I'm sorry about it. But I got to check. MacKenzie was gored to death, like he was jabbed by an angry bull." Then he showed her the picture of the double-bladed knife.

Jeff stared at it too and felt sick. It was stained with dried blood. The blood of his best friend. He felt lightheaded for a second, then looked at Robyn.

She'd gone as white as snow and was shaking a little. Without thinking, he put his arm around her to comfort her, and she clutched at his hand. Her own felt almost frozen.

The sheriff, naturally, had missed none of this. Like a vulture, he leaned closer to her. "Familiar, eh?"

Robyn finally nodded reluctantly. "My . . . my father," she said in an almost inaudible voice. "It's my father's knife."

EIGHT

LEO: *A changeable day. Good news and bad news intermix, and it's hard for you to know when you're ahead.*

Robyn stared at the sheriff, whose eyes gleamed at this piece of news. "Let me get this straight," he said slowly. "This knife is your father's? Not one like it, but this very one?"

Robyn wasn't sure what she should do. Would it get her father into trouble? But what could she possibly say? "That's his," she said dully. "It was made especially for him."

"Really? Was he planning on killing somebody?"

Furiously, she yelled, "My father wouldn't hurt anyone! He's—"

"Then why did he buy this loopy knife?" the sheriff snapped.

Jeff touched her arm gently. Robyn looked at him and

saw he was on her side. She felt glad for the support. Calming down, she explained, "He's in the S.C.A. and he wanted it for one of their functions."

"The what? Is that like the N.R.A. or I.R.A.?"

"Neither," she told him. "It's the Society for Creative Anachronism. They re-create the historical period of the Middle Ages at meetings. People dress as a person from those times. My father plays a blacksmith, and he had a friend make him the knife to make his costume look more interesting. He uses it in games to convince people who owe him money to pay up. It was just for fun. It was never meant to be used."

Putting the photo back in his pocket, Sheriff Adkins said dryly, "Well, it has been now. What say we take a drive and talk to your father?"

"Can I come too?" Jeff asked quickly. Robyn shot him a grateful look; the thought of going home in a police car with the sheriff on her own unnerved her.

The sheriff shrugged. "Suit yourself. Meet me outside in five minutes. I've got a few things to clear up." Then he left the room.

Jeff switched off the computer. "End of project for today," he said lightly. "You okay?"

"Not really," she answered honestly. "But I can take it. Thanks for offering to come with me. It's nice of you."

"That's okay," he told her.

Jeff fell silent, and she was lost in her own thoughts. *How had her father's knife been used to kill Alan?* she wondered. It made no sense. Then she realized that the sheriff might be thinking that her father might have been the killer! Which was flat-out impossible. Dad wasn't capable of doing anything like that.

But it was his knife, a whispering voice seemed to say in her mind. *Are you sure it wasn't him?*

No, it was ridiculous! Her father would explain everything when they got there. She wasn't betraying him, because there was nothing to betray.

So—why did she feel guilty?

They had to wait for the sheriff. Other students that were leaving circled well away from the official car that they were standing next to. Both Robyn and Jeff were watched on the sly, but nobody came any closer to them than they had to. Not even Debi, Dana, and Natalie, and that hurt.

Actually, there was no sign of her three friends, and Robyn realized that they'd probably already left. But, because she was depressed to begin with, even this seemed like a black mark against the day. She glared almost belligerently at the students who slunk past.

Were they afraid that they would get the plague? Or that they might get picked up for talking to two such hardened criminals? Robyn was appalled at the way she and Jeff were being deserted. *At least he stuck by me,* she thought.

The little voice in the back of her mind came back. *Are you sure he's coming along to help you?* it whispered. *Maybe he knows something about the murders and is checking up on the sheriff? Maybe he's the killer and wants to be certain the sheriff can't catch him.*

No! she said to it silently. *He's here to help me. That's all. He likes me.*

Seeming to sense her inner struggle, Jeff touched her

arm gently. "It's okay," he assured her. "Everything will work out fine. There's a simple explanation for everything, I'm sure."

But was there?

When they reached the Chantry house, Robyn used her key to let the sheriff, the silent deputy, and Jeff in with her. She called out to her father, but there was no reply.

"That's weird," she said. "He's always working at this time of day." She peered into the workshop, but there was no sign of him.

Jeff's eyebrows rose as he looked into the workshop and he whistled. "Is your father the one who makes these incredible things?"

"Yes."

He shook his head. "That's some skill. I didn't know your family had so much talent in it. I always loved these things. I've got a couple myself."

The sheriff grunted. "So—where's your father?"

Robyn was about to say that she didn't know, when she saw him—coming downstairs from his bedroom. He looked like he'd been sleeping. "Here I am," he said, rubbing the back of his neck. "What's wrong, Robyn?" He looked concerned. "Has there been some trouble?"

"You might say that," Sheriff Adkins said. "There was another murder last night."

"Right. That boy from the school." Mr. Chantry looked puzzled. "That's bad news. But what does that have to do with Robyn?"

"Not me, Dad," she said heavily. "You." She looked

at Jeff, and he gave her a quick, tense smile. "It was your knife that was used to kill him."

"What?" Mr. Chantry looked stunned. The sheriff showed him the photograph of the double-bladed knife. "Do you recognize this weapon?"

Mr. Chantry peered at it for a while before he seemed able to focus. Then, finally, he nodded. "I have one just like it," he acknowledged. "But mine is in here. Come on." He led the way into his candle room. Robyn and Jeff followed the sheriff in. Her father went to a cupboard and opened it. "Here's my costume," he said. "You know about the S.C.A.?"

"A little," the sheriff said.

"Well, I keep the knife with . . ." His voice trailed off, and he looked from the costume to the cupboard. "It's gone."

Raising his eyebrows, the sheriff said slowly, "I take it, then, that the murder weapon and your . . . missing . . . knife are one and the same."

"It does look like it," Mr. Chantry agreed in a small voice. "But it was in here the last time I looked."

"Which was?"

Robyn's father thought for a moment. "Saturday. I wore it to the shire meeting. Then when I came home, I put it away."

"Could anyone have taken the knife without your knowledge?"

Mr. Chantry shrugged. "Well, the cupboard is never locked. Anyone in the house, I suppose, could have taken it." Then, realizing what he had said, he added quickly, "Customers, I mean. People come here all the time to make orders or to buy samples. I have retailers in and out three, four times a day. Any one of them could have taken it when I wasn't looking."

"Provided that they knew you kept the knife there," the sheriff said. "Like anyone in your family." He glanced at Robyn again, and she shivered. "Well, I guess that's all for now. Maybe you would come down to the station and identify the knife formally for me. It's a nasty weapon. And maybe you could work up a list of the people who've been in and out of this workshop since you last saw the knife. More footwork for us, talking to them, but that's the job."

"That knife was never meant to be used," Mr. Chantry said.

"Then it's been abused." Sheriff Adkins looked at Robyn, then Jeff. "You two can take off—for now." He nodded at them, and then looked at Robyn's father and jerked his head.

Mr. Chantry sighed and turned to Robyn. "Better call your mother and tell her where I am. She'll probably want to close the shop and meet me there. Will you be okay, honey?"

"Of course." Robyn reached up and kissed his cheek. "I love you," she whispered.

"Likewise." He looked at Jeff, obviously wondering who he was.

"This is Jeff Goldstein," Robyn explained. "My science fair partner."

"Oh. The ner . . . computer whiz." Trying to cover up his slip of the tongue, he added, "Would you mind staying here with Robyn till I come back? If the killer's been here once, I'm not happy about leaving the place

65

unattended. And I'd feel better if there was someone with my daughter."

"Oh, sure," Jeff agreed. He had frowned at the slip, but his face was unreadable now. Robyn wondered if her father had insulted Jeff.

As soon as the police car pulled away, Robyn turned to Jeff. "You've been really nice," she told him. "But I really don't need protecting. If you'd rather not stay . . ."

"No, no, it's okay," he answered. "I promised your father I would." He glanced around uncertainly. "But if I could call my mom . . . she'll have a fit if I don't come home. Especially if she's heard about Alan."

"Sure." Robyn led him into the kitchen and gestured toward the wall phone. "Help yourself." He stood there, hesitating. Robyn realized he wanted privacy. "Uh—I'm just going to change my clothes. Back in a minute."

As she started upstairs, she heard him start dialing. *Why didn't he want to talk to his mother with me there?* she wondered. He was becoming more and more of an enigma all of the time. In her room, she quickly stripped off her skirt and top, then pulled on jeans and a T-shirt. Should she wait a little longer before going down?

Glancing at her desk, she saw her copy of William Vande Water's *Star Laws: The Forces That Guide Our Lives*. Scooping it up, she went downstairs. Jeff had already hung up when she arrived and was standing by the table looking uncomfortable.

"I thought you might like to look at this," she told him, handing him the book. "It's a really good guide to starting astrology. It might help you with the computer

66

programs we have to develop." Jeff took the book. "So, want a soda?" Robyn asked.

"Sure," he agreed. "Whatever you've got."

She poured them both glasses of cola and asked, "Did you get through to your mother?"

"Yes." He looked uneasy again. "My mother . . . worries a lot," he explained. "It's kind of embarrassing, really. But she means well."

"Parents can be like that," Robyn agreed.

"I'm sure your father will be fine," Jeff said.

"Why shouldn't he be?" she countered, perhaps too strongly. "He hasn't done anything. Somebody must have stolen that knife from him."

"Hey, I'm on your side," Jeff said. "I believe you. Besides, he'd have to be pretty stupid to use his own obviously unique knife to kill somebody with. And your father isn't dumb."

She nodded, glad of his support. Then, suddenly, she was struck by a very weird thought. "Jeff?" she asked, hardly daring to put it into words. "Do you remember what the sheriff said about Alan's murder?" She saw a wave of pain cross his face, and cursed herself for having forgotten that Alan was his best friend. "I'm sorry."

"It's okay," he said. "I have to face the fact that he's gone. Anyway, what do you mean?"

"Well," she replied, plowing on now, "he said that it looked like he'd been gored by a bull."

"So?"

"Alan was a Taurus."

Jeff shrugged stiffly. "Coincidence. Pretty bizarre, I agree, but that's it."

"No, it isn't." Certain she was onto something,

Robyn went on, "Jenny was strangled by a woollen scarf. Not silk or polyester, but wool. She was an Aries—the Ram. And both murders were done when their horoscopes said something bad would happen to them, exactly a week apart."

Jeff snorted, but good-naturedly. "That's weird, but there can't be anything to it."

"But Jeff—Aries and Taurus, in that order, are the first two signs of the Zodiac."

That made him think. Frowning, he muttered, "That's pretty weird." Then he stared at her. "You don't think . . . you know what it means, if you're right?"

"Yes." With a shiver of horror, Robyn said, "There will be at least ten more murders. One each week for each sign of the Zodiac. And the next victim will be a Gemini."

NINE

GEMINI: A day to be very careful. A cloud hangs over you, and you may be of two minds. The evening is especially bad for you.

"I think this New Age nuttiness has gone right to your brain," Natalie said firmly. She stared at Robyn and shook her head. "Come on—death by horoscopes? That's even dumber than the time you recalled your past life as a call girl in ancient Babylon."

"*Priestess*," Robyn said, a little annoyed. Natalie was starting to get on her nerves. "*Not* a hooker. There's a big difference. And what's so stupid about my theory? Jeff thinks it's unlikely, but possible."

Dana nudged Natalie in the ribs and gave her a very obvious wink. "Hear that—she's quoting Jeff Goldstein now. Sounds pretty serious to me."

"That's enough," Debi broke in, before Robyn had a chance to reply. "You two have been in a bad mood for a couple of weeks now, but I think it's time you stopped taking it out on other people. What's going on with you, anyway?" Her pretty face creased into a frown.

"Who are you?" Natalie asked. "Her keeper? If you ask me, it sounds like she's going to need one soon. Either that or a padded cell."

"Okay, fine," Robyn said coldly. "I've had it up to here with you." She glared at Natalie. "Friends like you nobody needs. When you feel like acting like a human being again, maybe I'll talk to you. Until then, stay out of my face." She spun on her heels and marched off down the corridor.

"Go cry on Jeff Goldstein's shoulder," Natalie called after her. "If he'll listen."

Debi ran after Robyn and caught up with her. "Ignore her," she advised. "I think she's just discovered PMS or something."

"Why is she acting like this?" Robyn asked. "She was always a motor mouth, but she's been so obnoxious the last few weeks."

"Search me," Debi replied. Then she saw Joe Butler leaning against the lockers, reading the school paper. "Is work that slow, Joe?" she asked with a smile.

He looked up, guiltily. "Oh, it's you." He shrugged. "I like to keep up with the newspaper," he told her. "School spirit and all. I always had a hankering to write, but never made it. Never really lucky, I guess."

"Oh, I don't know," Debi said, grinning. "Where else could you work and see so many gorgeous girls in one day?"

He grinned back. "You may have a point there," he agreed. Then he looked over their shoulders. "Oops—

it's Traynor. I'd better get busy." He shot off down the corridor as fast as his bad leg would let him.

"Ah, Ms. Chantry!" the science teacher called. "A moment, if you please." Robyn sighed, but they waited for him to catch up with them. "I've been meaning to ask you how your science fair project is going."

"Better than I expected," she answered honestly. "Jeff's pretty smart, and he's getting really interested in our horoscope program." She smiled. "Thanks for putting us together, Mr. Traynor. I really am learning a lot."

Mr. Traynor looked surprised and pleased. "It's all a matter of motivation and application," he told her. "Anything can be interesting if you believe in your mind that it can be." He nodded, then moved off.

"Sounds like he learned his philosophy at the feet of Walt Disney," muttered Debi. "He'll have you wishing on a star next, and shouting, *I can fly! I can fly!*"

Robyn giggled. "Still, he did do me a favor," she admitted. "I might actually pass science. And I am learning a lot from Jeff."

Debi gave her a funny look. "You're not actually getting interested in him, are you?"

"No," replied Robyn defensively. "But he's pretty neat, when you get to know him." Honestly, why did her friends find her friendship with Jeff so fascinating? He was a nice guy. They had to work together. Period.

"Oh, he's okay," Debi admitted. "As long as you're just friends."

Suspecting something, Robyn stared at her friend. "What do you know that I don't?"

Debi glanced at her watch. "Come on, we'd better

head home. I'll tell you on the way." Frowning, Robyn followed her out the school doors.

"Jeff lives just a couple of blocks from our house," Debi said once they were on their way. "But we hardly ever see him anywhere. He stays home almost all the time with his mother."

"A mama's boy?" guessed Robyn. "Like Derek Vine?"

Debi shook her head. "Nothing like that. But—his mother's crazy. She's been in and out of mental hospitals for years."

Robyn felt cold. "Really? How awful. The poor thing."

"Not so poor," Debi answered. "It's kind of the local scandal, but not many people remember it. Jeff's dad left home about ten years ago, the same time that his mother went to the hospital for the first time. And get this. She tried to kill him."

"What?" Robyn was shocked.

"Yeah. Apparently she freaked out one night and went for him with a carving knife. Got one good stab in before Jeff could drag her away. He was only seven, you know. It never went to court, but Jeff's dad left town and his mother was sent off for treatment. She's been in and out since then. Jeff's really embarrassed and sensitive about the whole thing, and he's never had any friends over to his place."

"That's terrible," Robyn said, her heart going out to both Jeff and his mother. "So that's why we always work at school."

"If I were you," advised Debi, "I wouldn't get too close to him. Jeff's bad news. He's probably just as cracked as his mother."

"That's not true," Robyn said hotly. "He's a lot more together than most people I know." But inside her, that small voice was back, dragging out terrible thoughts: *He's just as crazy as his mother—and she attacked her husband with a knife. Somebody attacked Alan MacKenzie with a knife . . .*

No matter how hard she tried, she couldn't get those thoughts out of her mind.

Natalie was in her room, trying to do her homework. It was almost nine, and dark outside. She closed the curtains and chewed nervously at her fingernails, waiting. It was bound to start soon. It was impossible for her to get her work done—the tension of waiting was too much.

Finally, about ten minutes later, it started. She heard the sound of glass breaking downstairs and her father's drink-slurred voice. Then her mother's, raised in anger, and another sound of breaking glass.

No matter how hard she wished, it never went away.

Her father had lost his job three weeks before. Bitter, he had started drinking. He was convinced he was too old to start again. Her mother, terrified of their shrunken income, had started to nag at him.

Then the fighting had begun.

Tears welling up in her eyes, Natalie could hear them downstairs yelling. Soon the rougher side would begin. She closed her door and threw herself onto her bed, crying. It had been a hellish two weeks. She had always loved both her adoptive parents, and they adored her, she knew. But now the cracks in the happy family had begun to show, and she was terrified that it would mean

73

a breakup. She couldn't take it. What would happen to her?

She lost herself in tears.

Outside, in the night, he waited. In the shadows by the garage he stood and listened. The sound of breaking glass brought a nod of grim satisfaction. He'd been very precise about this. Having decided that Natalie Byrnes was next, he had then carefully checked her habits. Unlike his last two victims, Natalie hardly ever went out at night. But that was no real problem.

He would simply have to go in after her.

He heard the yelling begin and knew that it was time.

Pulling the screwdriver from his pocket, he worked on the lock to the side door. It took him just a few seconds to shatter the wood around the lock, and he did it with hardly a sound. Any noise he had made would be masked by the fight going on inside, anyway.

The door opened to his touch and he slipped the screwdriver back into his pocket. He glided across the dark garage and opened the inside door a crack. As he had expected, it was unlocked and opened into the kitchen. Quickly, he went in.

There was nobody in the room. He could hear the sound of pouring drinks and cursing from the front of the house. The stairs up to Natalie's room were close. As long as they didn't squeak, he'd be fine. If they did . . . well, he was certain that they wouldn't. He was the living will of the Zodiac, and this was his mission. The Zodiac would not allow him to be discovered before his task was accomplished.

He moved quietly up the stairs. Only one door up-stairs had a sliver of light showing under it.

She was in there. The time had come.

He took the coil of wire out of his pocket. This time, silence was the most important thing. Natalie had to die —but very quietly.

All cried out, Natalie stood in front of the full-length mirror on the back of her closet door and dabbed at her eyes with a tissue. Voices from downstairs told her that the arguing was still going on. Soon enough, she knew she would hear the first blow. Each time that she did, she cringed as if she was the one who had been struck, who had been hurt.

Instead, she heard a faint sound at the door. She turned with a smile, hopeful that maybe tonight would be different, tonight the fighting would stop.

She was right.

Tonight was different. And, for her at least, the fight-ing stopped.

Permanently.

Ed Byrnes poured himself another scotch, ignoring the screaming, nagging voice of his wife. He took a deep swill, feeling the euphoria wash over him. Life was one huge pain, but at least in drink there was numbness. He could feel it working—his toes had gone already. Soon the rest of his body and mind would follow them.

Then he would be free.

Instead, there was a sound of a crash from upstairs. Dimly, through his scotch-misted mind, he wondered if it was from Natalie's room. Maybe she had fallen down or something. He and his wife looked at each other, their anger still frozen on their faces. A measure of his concern for his daughter still survived the drunken attack on his senses, and he lurched toward the stairs to see what was going on. It took him three attempts to make the first step, but his momentum carried him up from there. Behind him, he could hear his wife's footsteps on the stairs. She was muttering about Natalie.

Mr. Byrnes hit his daughter's bedroom door, unable to stop, and fell through as it swung open. As he toppled over, he saw several things, none of them too clearly.

First was Natalie, slumped against her mirror, her face a terrible shade of blue. Around her neck, blood dripping from it, was a length of thin, shiny wire.

Then he saw someone else, standing by the open window. Just a dark, fuzzy shape, with something in his hands.

Finally, he saw a bright, blinding flash from whatever it was that the intruder held.

Then he hit the floor. By the time he pushed himself up and could see through the yellow haze of the afterimage, the intruder was gone.

But Natalie wasn't—except in the final, most terrible sense of that word.

He screamed out in pain, and heard a weird echo— his wife's matching scream. Then there was only oblivion.

TEN

AQUARIUS: A shared secret will bring you closer to a loved one, but your friendship could be endangered if you can't control your ego.

Jeff stared in shock at the television screen. He'd only turned it on to hear the day's weather report while he fixed himself breakfast, but had seen Natalie Byrnes's face staring back at him. The woman reporter giving the gruesome details of the slaying seemed oblivious to the reactions her words might cause.

"—head almost severed from her body by a wire noose," the sincere reporter was saying into a micro-phone, standing outside of the Byrneses' house. "This is the third time in less than a month that a teenager has been brutally murdered in what has been thought of as a stereotypical sleepy little town. Are we in the midst of a crime wave? I spoke with investigating officer Sheriff William Adkins."

The picture changed to show a taped conversation with the sadly familiar face of the sheriff. The reporter, in her usual confrontational style, asked, "Three teens in four weeks, Sheriff—and no leads to go on?"

"Look, ma'am," the sheriff replied, "first off, if I had any leads, I wouldn't air them so the perpetrator could know. Second, if I didn't have any leads, I wouldn't let the killer know that, either. Third, there's nothing to prove that the murders were all done by the same person. Each case had a different style about it. And fourth, if you don't take that thing out of my face, there'll be another death." He smiled. "Only everyone will know who killed *you*, 'cause it'll be on national TV. Out of my way, ma'am—some of us have real work to do."

The picture returned to that of the reporter, outside the Byrneses' house again. "As you can see, the sheriff seems to have no clues to go on in the three cases. As to whether there will be more murders from the killer the news is already dubbing 'The Teen Terror'—only time will tell."

Jeff slammed off the set, irritated by the reporter's seemingly casual approach. A girl was dead, and this was just grist for the news mill. Jeff had never particularly liked Natalie, but he was hurt and scared by her death. Three in a month . . . How many more were there to come?

Then it hit him: Natalie had been a friend of Robyn's. Did she know about the murder yet? This was going to hit her really hard, he knew. He wondered if he should call her and let her know—or would that be a mistake? Maybe she already knew. Maybe he'd get her so upset that she'd never speak to him again.

Well, that wasn't much to risk. He still hadn't worked up enough courage to be anything more than casually friendly. He didn't even know if she liked him at all. Maybe she was just being tolerant, because they had to do this project together. She'd probably laugh herself silly if he asked her out. Still, he could at least talk to her.

He picked up the kitchen phone and dialed her number. He'd memorized it weeks ago.

A woman answered. "Mrs. Chantry?" he asked, then plunged on. "This is Jeff Goldstein."

"Jeff?" After a second: "Oh, you're Robyn's partner in the science thing. Hang on, and I'll get her for you."

"No," he said quickly. "I mean, maybe you'd better pass the news on for me." Now it had come to it, he simply didn't have the courage to tell her himself. "I just saw on TV that a friend of hers was killed last night. Natalie Byrnes."

"Oh, God." There was a pause, then: "Yes, you're right. I'd better tell her." The line went dead.

Replacing the receiver, Jeff looked at it somewhat guiltily. Well, he'd chickened out of that one. Chock up another lost opportunity for Jeff Goldstein. Was he always going to be such a wimp? "Faint heart never won fair lady," he said, repeating Alan's advice. Only now Alan was dead. And Natalie. And Jenny Warren.

He stopped and stared at the phone.

This was getting too sick, but . . .

They were all not only in the same school, but the same year. And they all knew one another. What were the odds of a random killer picking three victims like that? Pretty near zero.

Despite the sheriff's words, the deaths *had* to be connected. But how? And why?

The phone rang.

He stared at it, inexplicably scared. It was too early in the day for a telephone solicitor. Virtually nobody else ever called.

Hesitantly, he reached out and picked it up. "Hello?"

"Jeff? It's Robyn." Her voice sounded cracked; she'd obviously been crying. "I want to talk to you at school. Be by the lockers." Then the phone went dead.

He stood there, holding the receiver until it beeped loudly to be replaced. Then he set it down and finished getting ready for school in a rush.

Why did she want to see him? Was she mad at him for breaking the news? Was she going to tell him that she wouldn't work with him anymore? Was she—

"Who was that calling, Jeff?"

He looked up. His mother was in the doorway, nervously wringing her hands together. Her eyes darted from side to side.

"Just one of my school friends, Mom," he replied gently. "Nothing to be worried about."

"You're sure it wasn't your father, dear?"

"Quite sure, Mom." He took her arm and led her back to the den. "You just rest. I'm going to school now. Okay?"

She sat in the rocker and nodded absently. "Yes, that's fine. I'll just wait here for you."

With a sigh, he left the room. His mother—forty-one years old. Mental age of about fourteen. And with her white hair and stooped body, she looked almost sixty.

And she was still terrified that one day his father would come home again.

When he reached school, Jeff shot indoors. There was no sign of Robyn yet by the lockers. He was glad he'd reached them first, but also uncertain and nervous. He had longer to imagine all kinds of reasons why she wanted to see him and to panic over the possibilities.

"That's not your locker," said a quiet voice. Jeff almost jumped, and saw it was the custodian, Joe.

"Uh, no, I know," he said. "I'm just waiting for a friend."

Joe looked at him suspiciously. "We've been having some trouble with those lockers. Like someone's been messing with them."

"It wasn't me," Jeff assured him. "I'm not touching anything. I'm just waiting for Robyn Chantry, that's all."

The custodian didn't seem to believe this, but then Robyn's voice cut in.

"That's right, Joe. I asked him to meet me."

Jeff turned around and saw that Robyn and Debi were coming down the corridor. Joe gave him another suspicious look, then nodded and moved on. Jeff saw that both girls showed evidence of crying—red eyes and puffy faces.

"Are you okay?" he asked gently.

Robyn shook her head. "No. I'm not." She swallowed. "But I can go on. I'm—I'm glad you called with the news. I wouldn't have wanted to hear it at school."

"I wish I had had a better reason to call you," he said.

"I wish you had, too." She sighed, and her body

shook. Jeff could see that she was still on the verge of tears. "Anyway, do you remember that I said the next victim would be a Gemini? Well, Natalie was born June second. She was a Gemini."

"Then your theory about a Zodiac link looks like it's true," he said softly. "But—well, uh . . . I heard that Natalie was strangled. That's not in keeping with the sign, is it?" He didn't like bringing up the grisly details of Natalie's death. Robyn winced and Debi sniffled, but they didn't break into tears. For that, at least, he was glad. He wouldn't have known what to do if they had.

Robyn unfolded the morning newspaper. "I know. But it says here that she was killed in front of her mirror. Like there were two bodies."

"Gemini—the twins," Jeff breathed, taking the paper from her. He started to scan it quickly for anything else he could learn. "This is getting just too freaky."

"To be honest, it's scaring the hell out of me," Robyn told him.

"It's going to get worse," he replied. "Think about it —all three victims were in our year. We knew all of them."

Debi shuddered. "That's right . . ." She looked like she was about to throw up. "What are you trying to say?"

Jeff shifted uncomfortably. Even worse than Debi crying would be to have her be sick. "Uh, well—it looks like the killer really has to be someone from our year. Someone who knew the Zodiac signs of the people killed. That's not exactly common knowledge, is it?"

Robyn caught on instantly. "The police think it was Derek Vine. You don't?"

"No. I mean, let's face it—he hates this astrology stuff. Even if he wanted to kill people—and I don't think he would—why would he use a Zodiac method?"

Robyn thought for a moment. "Maybe to express his disdain at horoscopes?"

"I think that's reaching a bit," Jeff said. "Just because he doesn't like astrology doesn't mean he'd kill people."

"No . . ." Robyn agreed slowly. "But if he had grudges against people, maybe he'd get rid of them in a pattern. I mean, we know he argued with Jenny *and* Alan. And he blamed the horoscope for Jenny's death. He didn't know I'd written them—maybe he thought it was Natalie?"

"That doesn't make sense, either," Debi objected. "If he killed Jenny, why would he blame Natalie for doing it?"

"If he's crazy, who knows?"

Jeff shook his head firmly. "This isn't getting us anywhere. We need more proof, or at least more concrete information." He made a sudden decision that he was afraid could be a mistake. "Robyn, can you come over to my house after school? I think maybe we can get a lead on all of this." He turned to Debi. "You can come too, if you want."

Robyn nodded without hesitating. "Okay, if you think it'll help get whoever is killing our friends."

"I'm in," Debi added firmly.

"Okay," Jeff said. The decision was made now. All he had to do was go through with it. To his surprise, it felt good to have finally made a commitment to action.

If only he didn't live to regret it.

ELEVEN

LEO: Surprises are in store for you. Some are good, some bad. But changes will occur in your life.

"I don't believe it," Debi said to Robyn when they were on their way to class. "Jeff Goldstein asked us over." She gave Robyn a funny look. "He must really like you."

"It's no big deal," Robyn replied. "I've been to lots of people's houses."

"Yeah," her friend agreed. "But Jeff hasn't had anyone over to his place in years. I've heard that he usually stops people from coming in."

"You're just dying of curiosity, aren't you?" Robyn realized. "Well, you'll find out the secrets of the Goldstein house today. But you behave yourself."

Debi smiled. "You guys are getting to be real pals, aren't you?"

"Not exactly," Robyn lied, unwilling to admit it. "But he's not the nerd I thought he was."

"You'd better watch it. It's the quiet ones who are trouble."

"You're full of wise old sayings," Robyn said. "Have you been getting them from my mother?"

The day went slowly. No matter how hard she tried, Robyn couldn't keep the aching pain she felt about Natalie's death out of her mind. She felt especially bad that the last time she'd talked to Natalie, they had fought. She hadn't meant that to be their last conversation. And she wished that they'd been able to make up again. But it would never happen.

She wasn't the only one to feel the loss. Even when she herself was trying not to cry, she saw that Debi and Dana were both in the same state. In fact, most of the students were very subdued. Some, she knew, were silent because of their sorrow over Natalie. Others because they were terrified that they'd be the next victim of this Teen Terror.

Everyone avoided going anywhere near Derek Vine.

Derek's bad temper seemed to have settled over him permanently. He coldly ignored the accusing glances that were shot his way, but Robyn was certain that he couldn't be anywhere near as thick-skinned as he pretended. But was he just angry because he was falsely accused, or because he had been correctly identified as the killer?

Adding to everything else, each time Robyn looked out of the classroom window, she could see a police car sitting in the street, with a man in it. Watching the school to protect it? To keep an eye on the prime suspect? Derek's eyes kept creeping back to the car, too.

Finally, though, school was over. Silently, still hurting, Debi went with Robyn to their lockers. While they waited for Jeff to arrive, Joe Butler drifted past, limping as usual, carrying his tools. He gave them a somber nod.

"Bad thing, what happened to Natalie Byrnes," he said. "I know she was a friend of yours. I'm sorry."

"Thanks, Joe," Robyn said. "It's really been a heavy few weeks. You think they'll ever catch the killer?"

"Hard to say." He scratched his head. "Guess it depends on luck. Most of life does. Haven't had much of it myself. Like you girls—you'll be off to college, or out into nice jobs when this year's done. You'll all do better than me, I'll bet."

"Not all of us," Debi said softly. "Natalie, Jenny, and Alan won't."

"No," he agreed, shaking his head. "It's a bad thing." He looked up and saw Jeff coming down the corridor. "You girls waiting for him?"

"Yes," replied Robyn.

Joe's eyes darkened. "You watch out for him," he warned them. "I knew his father. A bad sort. Like father, like son, that's what they say. Just be careful." Before they could say anything, he moved off without another glance.

What did he mean by that? Robyn wondered. What did he know that she didn't? She'd known Joe vaguely for years. He and her mother had gone to this school together. Joe had kept in loose contact with her family since he'd returned to town and become the school custodian. He was into health food and stopped by the shop a lot. Mrs. Chantry reckoned he kept hoping that a good diet might help his bad leg. Robyn had always been polite to him, even if she sometimes found Joe's intense manner a bit off-putting. But he seemed concerned for her and Debi, even if his concern was misplaced.

Jeff hurried over. "Sorry I'm late," he apologized. "Mr. Traynor kept me a while. Ready?" The girls nodded and Jeff led them out of school. "It's not far. We can walk. I thought we could talk on the way."

"About what?" Debi asked.

Jeff looked very uneasy. "Well," he said finally, "about my mother." He looked at Debi. "You live near me. I'm sure you've heard all sorts of stories."

Debi looked as if she was about to deny it, but then she nodded. "Yeah. People do talk a lot."

"Don't I know it." Jeff sighed, then appeared to gather up his resolve. "I guess they all say she's crazy?"

"Something like that," Debi agreed with embarrassment, looking down at the sidewalk.

Robyn could feel for what Jeff was going through. He must feel really awkward, and was clearly not very good at expressing his feelings or exposing his secrets.

"She's *not* crazy," he said. "Well, not in the way most people mean, anyway. She's just childlike. You can have a conversation with her, and she's perfectly okay. She can take care of herself. It's just that she's still like a kid." He was very uncomfortable, laying himself open like this.

"It must be hard on you," Robyn said sympathetically.

He gave her a smile of thanks. "Not too bad," he replied. "I've gotten pretty used to it over the years. But

—well, other people get kind of uncomfortable around her. Like they're scared she'll go berserk and attack them or something."

Debi gave him a look. "Well, she *did* attack your father. That's why they put her in the home to begin with, isn't it? And no one saw your dad again."

"No!" He flushed. "I mean, not like that. It wasn't her fault." He took a deep breath and let it out very slowly. "You never knew my dad. He was a monster. He had an uncontrollable temper, and then he'd hit Mom and me too. Broke my arm one time. Mom used to be real scared for me. But she was terrified of leaving Dad. He always warned her that if she tried it, he'd hunt us down and kill us."

"How horrible," Robyn whispered. What a contrast to her family!

"Yeah, it was pretty awful. Well, that last night, he was worse than we'd ever seen him. We never knew why, but he was in one of his rages again. I don't even remember what it was, but something I did upset him, and he backhanded me across the room." He was lost in his memories now. "I hit the wall and was really dazed. They told me later that I had a mild concussion. I couldn't move at all, just lay there.

"Mom was really pale, terrified, and she started screaming that he'd killed me. He slapped her. She fell over and hit her head. Dad must have been scared that he'd killed her or something. There was blood all over the place. But Mom wasn't dead. Instead, she had grabbed up a kitchen knife, and when Dad went over to see what he'd done, she stabbed him. She was just so scared that he would kill her if he got hold of her.

"Dad sort of choked and fell over, this knife sticking out of him. I don't really remember what happened much after that. The neighbors had heard all the noise and called the cops. When they arrived, they called for an ambulance, and we were all rushed off to the hospital.

"Later, it turned out that Mom had suffered some brain damage when she fell. She's never really been right since. Grandma moved in with us and helped to look after Mom. Then, when Grandma died a couple of years ago, I took over. Mom's still terrified that one day Dad'll come back to try to finish killing us."

Jeff was silent, lost in his memories of that horrible night. Robyn, feeling sympathy for him wash over her, reached out and touched his hand. "Is that likely?"

If he noticed her touch, he didn't react. "No." He shook his head. "Dad was dead by the time the ambulance arrived. The police decided not to press charges, since Mom was so badly hurt. They knew she'd been provoked a lot and that she wasn't mentally competent to stand trial. They told her he was dead, but she never could believe it. She still worries about visitors, thinking it might be Dad. So we don't have people over much."

Robyn couldn't think of anything to say at first. No wonder Jeff was such a loner! He'd been driven to it. "Will she be all right with us there?" she asked.

"I think so," he replied. "You're both girls, and that should help. But if she gets worked up, you'll have to leave. She gets anxiety attacks sometimes, and they're pretty hard to control."

Robyn nodded. "Understood." Then, to her own surprise, she added, "Is that why you've never had a girlfriend?" she asked. "Because you're afraid of your mother's reaction?"

He looked at her, his eyes very desolate. "No," he said softly. "That's not it. I'm afraid of my own reactions."

"What?"

He looked down at the sidewalk. "I'm scared that I'd be just like my father. Like father, like son. I never want to put anyone through what Mom and I went through."

Realizing that he was perfectly serious about this, Robyn grabbed his shoulder, jerking him to a stop. He looked up at her, startled. "Stop that!" she said firmly. "You're being so dumb. You're much too smart and kind to ever end up like that." She shook her head. "Here you are, making fun of me for believing that the stars have an influence on us. But look at you—scared that your father's temper is in your blood! Which one of us is the stupid one?"

He looked at her, amazed. "You really believe that?"

"Yes, I do," she said hotly. "And if you had an ounce of sense in your skull, you'd believe it, too. As long as you can even worry about hurting people like your father did, you'll never do it. Because you know the pain of being on the other side of the fence."

It was as if she'd lifted a great load from his soul. "You really believe that," he said. He nodded in amazement. "If you can, then I can."

Despite the events of the past few weeks, Robyn felt pretty good. She seemed to have given Jeff a new lease on life. He appeared more self-assured, as though all he had ever needed was someone else to have a little faith in him.

The three of them walked on until they came to a small ranch house. It was neatly kept and trimmed in blue and white. The garden was tidy and flowers dotted the place. Obviously, Jeff was pretty handy around the house. He led them to the door and opened it with his key.

"Hi, Mom," he called. "I'm home! And there's somebody here for you to meet."

After a moment, Mrs. Goldstein moved slowly from the study. She looked relieved to see that there was no man with her son. Beaming brightly, she held out her hand. "Hello."

Robyn shook her hand. "Hello."

Mrs. Goldstein examined her carefully. "You're very pretty," she said finally. "Are you Jeff's girlfriend?"

"No, Mom," said Jeff gently. "She's my partner in the science fair at school, that's all."

That was true enough, but Robyn wished somehow that he hadn't said it. Why did it make her feel sad inside?

"Pity," sighed Mrs. Goldstein. "I keep telling him to find a nice girl. And you look like a very nice girl to me. Well, perhaps one day he'll listen to his mother." Then she shifted her attention to Debi, who stood, embarrassed, in the background. "Don't fidget, girl. It's bad manners." She peered closer. "You look sort of familiar to me."

"I'm Debi Smolinske," she answered quietly.

"Smolinske?" Mrs. Goldstein thought for a moment. "I went to school with a Peter Smolinske once."

"My father," Debi explained.

Mrs. Goldstein nodded, then leaned forward. "Watch

him," she said secretively. "He's far too fond of his money, that one." Then she smiled at her son. "You'll look after these two young ladies, won't you?"

"Definitely!" he promised. "We're just going to my room, okay?"

She nodded. "I'll make a snack. Off you go."

Jeff led the way down the hall, smiling. "You made my mom's day," he told Robyn. "She hasn't been this cheerful for a long time."

"She seems very nice," Robyn said politely. She didn't add: *And not really all that crazy.* She couldn't help but wonder, though, just how stable Jeff was himself. A father who abused his wife and son, and a mother who'd killed her husband . . . Where did that leave Jeff?

He threw open the door to his room. "In we go."

The three of them entered his room, and the two girls both gasped in astonishment.

TWELVE

AQUARIUS: *Time to rethink some of your priorities. Your friendship will prove very valuable to others today.*

There was a small bed along the near wall, and a walk-in closet. There was a single window on the side wall. The rest of the room was filled with computer equipment. There was a monitor, keyboard, and large processor on a wooden desk, and over it a hutch filled with computer disks. There were books, boxes of programs, and several pieces of equipment that neither girl recognized. Debi whistled.

"What is all this stuff?"

Jeff smiled. "A step or ten up from the school computer," he said proudly. "Grandma left me a small fortune when she died, and I've invested it in my computer." He crossed to the desk and started the monitor up. "I've got it hooked up to a laser printer for print-outs, and a pretty powerful modem for networking. That came in handy last night."

The monitor lit up, and he started to type commands, then paused. "Uh . . . I should tell you that what I've done isn't strictly legal. So don't tell anyone about this, okay?"

"I don't think anyone would understand me," Debi answered. "I don't understand it myself."

"What did you do?" Robyn asked, more to the point.

"I used the modem to link up with the school computer," Jeff admitted. "I found out the password from Traynor's files and accessed all of the student files."

He had finished typing. A small device by the keyboard lit up, and then information began scrolling over the monitor. After a second, he tapped in some more information, and everything stopped. "Okay, I'm in the private files of the student body," he said. He glanced at Robyn. "I used it to check your information about the murders, and so far you're right on the money."

"So now what?" Debi asked, unable to figure out what was happening.

"Well, if Robyn's right," replied Jeff, "then we can discover who's likely to be the next victim. First, since all of the other victims have been from our year, I think we can assume that the next one will be too." He typed this into the computer. "Then it must be the next sign of the Zodiac—Cancer. Anything else we can be fairly sure of?"

Robyn frowned. "Well, one thing did occur to me. The first victim was female, the second male, and the third female."

Nodding, Jeff typed again. "So let's assume that the next one will be male. It makes sense. This killer seems to be working along a pattern. Now, I execute the command—" He typed in a final line and sat back.

The printer hummed, and a few seconds later it spat out a sheet of paper. Jeff grabbed it and held it so they could all see it.

There were eight names on it—Will Best, Tim Finnegan, Ed Gundlach, Peter Harrison, Sean O'Farrell, Ryan Sonderberg, Hal Taylor, and James Walsh. They all stared at it silently.

"Okay," Robyn said. "So if we're right, one of them is likely to be the next victim. But we don't know when—or how. So what do we do now?"

"There's only one thing we can do," Jeff said. "Hand this over to the police and tell them what we've figured out. Maybe they can keep an eye on these eight people."

Debi frowned. "That's a lot of guys to watch for an indefinite time," she pointed out. "And the sheriff only has a couple of men."

"Well, if he warns the kids involved, they might take precautions," Robyn suggested. "And I'm sure their parents would."

"Right," Jeff agreed. "Besides, we can't keep this to ourselves. But there's no need for you two to get involved any more. I'll go along myself and tell them about it."

There was a knock on the door and Mrs. Goldstein popped her head in. "Come have a snack," she said brightly.

* * *

Half an hour later, Debi and Robyn were on their way home together. Jeff was on his way to the sheriff's office. After a while, Robyn nudged Debi. "You're very quiet."

Starting, Debi looked at her. "I guess I am."

"That's not like you. Thinking about Natalie?"

"Not exactly." Unsure how to tactfully broach the subject, Debi blurted out, "Just promise me you and Jeff are just science partners—not anything more—not close friends."

"What?" Robyn looked stunned. "What are you talking about? I thought you liked Jeff."

"Think about what we know about the killer," Debi said hurriedly. "He's got access to private information about students. The students being killed are all in our year. Derek Vine isn't the only person who can carry a grudge, you know."

"Are you trying to say *Jeff* might be the killer?" asked Robyn, with dangerous quiet in her voice.

"You just saw yourself that he's tapped into the school records. He knows anything he wants to find out."

"He only did it yesterday."

Debi wasn't convinced. "So he says. But he *could* have done it months ago." She pressed on. "Natalie laughed in his face just a couple of days ago, and she was pretty mean to him for a long time. Alan MacKenzie was his best friend. If Jeff had a secret to hide, Alan was the most likely to have found it out."

"And Jenny Warren?"

Shrugging, Debi admitted, "I can't see why he'd have it in for her. But he might have a reason that we just don't know."

Robyn glared at her friend. "He's *not* a killer."

"Maybe not consciously," Debi agreed. "But . . . well, he told us that he'd been beaten by his father as a kid, and seen his mother kill his dad. Maybe that concussion he suffered affected his mind? Maybe he's living out his father's violence against other kids?"

Robyn went red. "Debi Smolinske, that's the meanest thing I've ever heard anyone ever say! I'm ashamed of you! Jeff's a nice guy, and I like him. I'm not going to listen to any more of your awful ideas."

"Maybe I'm wrong," Debi said reluctantly. "It's just an idea. I hope I am—for your sake."

Robyn gave her another look—but this time, mixed with the anger, there was a hint of doubt. Debi hated to ruin her friend's happiness, but sooner that than have her end up a victim, too.

THIRTEEN

SCORPIO: A day of questions—you ask and are asked more than you can answer. A time to search your soul for goals and intentions.

Derek sat in the sheriff's office, nervously waiting. It was a large, open room. A young woman in a police uniform sat at one of the three desks, typing away, her eyes fixed on the papers she was processing. The other two desks were unmanned, but filled with file folders, papers, and empty polystyrene coffee cups. From the rear office, he could hear his mother and Pastor Williams talking in low tones with Sheriff Adkins.

His mother had finally convinced the pastor to come along on Derek's behalf to talk to the police. She was convinced that her son was innocent of any crime. That made her almost the only person in town who was.

It was hard on Derek. Fear, worry, and doubt were gnawing at his mind and soul. What was going to happen to him? Was he going to get railroaded for the murders, simply because there were no other suspects?

He'd done a lot of thinking and listening to music lately, trying to calm down and find some answers. It had been bad enough having Jenny murdered—he still missed her so much. But to be unjustly accused of her murder was almost more than he could take. He'd done a lot of praying, but it was hard for him. Even in church, he knew, there were accusing eyes staring at him. Did they all think he was really a killer?

No matter how much he prayed, it seemed as if God had turned a deaf ear to him. Was this all the good being a Christian did for him? What was the point of it, if this could happen to him?

The door to the office opened and Pastor Williams came out. He was a tall man and an imposing and often fiery speaker in church. But now he looked shorter, as if beaten down by the cares of his flock. His thinning hair was almost all gray, even though he was only in his mid-forties.

He came to sit by Derek. "Your mother and the sheriff are still having words," he said. "But I doubt either will change their minds."

"It doesn't look good for me, huh?"

Pastor Williams managed a weak smile. "The sheriff admitted that he has no more than circumstantial evidence to link you to the first two deaths. And, aside from the fact that you are without any witnesses to your whereabouts, nothing at all linking you to the latest murder. However, he feels that there may be methods still to be explored that will result in your arrest. You are, I'm afraid, still his number-one suspect."

In a sudden burst of anger, Derek asked bitterly, "How could God let this happen?"

The pastor stared at him mildly. "Do you mean the murders, or your being accused of them? Either way, I don't think that God should be blamed."

"I can't think of anyone better to blame," Derek said honestly. He expected a rebuke, but instead Pastor Williams sighed and leaned back in his chair.

"We all doubt God at times, Derek," he said. "Never more so than when innocent people die—when they are brutally murdered. How could a God of love allow this to happen? I wish that there were simple answers that would make you and me, and all the world, happy. But there aren't."

"Then what good is God?" asked Derek impatiently.

"He is there to comfort us," the pastor replied. "He has suffered, too. I know you loved Jenny, but God loves her much more than we can. He sorrowed when she died, more than you can. Our pains break His heart. And, don't forget, His son was murdered, too. Trust me, God understands your pain and sympathizes with it. He will come to you, when you let him. But He cannot come while there is anger in your heart. The fire of anger prevents you from seeing Him."

"But—I can't stop being angry," Derek objected. "I'm being unjustly accused of killing Jenny—and Alan, and now Natalie. Of course I'm angry!"

"It's only human to be angry. But we're not called to be human, Derek. We're called to be holy. Remember, when Jesus was falsely accused of crimes, and when he was killed, he only said *forgive them—they don't understand what they are doing.* Try to feel like that, too. Let

100

the anger go and try to feel God at work. Only then can you know any peace."

Before Derek could reply, the door to the office opened and Jeff Goldstein walked in. He seemed surprised to see Derek, and came over. "You okay?" he asked.

"Wonderful," Derek sighed. "I just love being a murder suspect."

Jeff shrugged. "I know it doesn't mean much," he said. "But I don't think you could be a murderer."

Amazed, Derek stared at Jeff. "You're wrong," he replied. "It means a lot to have someone believe in me. Thanks." His heart felt a little lighter. *There's somebody who isn't accusing me!* Maybe Pastor Williams was right.

The door to the inner office opened and Mrs. Vine left, followed closely by Sheriff Adkins. Neither of them looked happy.

"Come, Derek," Mrs. Vine said frostily. "It's time we left."

"Excuse me," Jeff said politely, "but he might like to hear what I've got to say to the sheriff."

Derek's mother eyed Jeff suspiciously. "Why?"

"Yes, son," the sheriff asked. "What's eating you?"

Jeff pulled a list of names from his pocket. "I've been doing research on the murders, Sheriff," he explained. "I think that the killer is using a sort of Zodiac motif. And that eliminates Derek."

"What are you talking about?"

Jeff turned to Derek. "What's the astrological sign after Cancer?"

"I've no idea," answered Derek. "That's superstitious nonsense."

"Well," Sheriff Adkins drawled, "it appears we agree on one thing, at least." He turned back to Jeff. "Care to explain?"

"Derek doesn't know the Zodiac," Jeff pointed out. "But the killings are all related to their signs." He explained the theory he and Robyn had worked out, without mentioning her name. Then he handed over the list of eight names. "Those are the students with the highest chance of being the next victim," he said. "I think they should be warned, and maybe guarded. I don't know when the killer is likely to strike again, though."

The sheriff had clearly had enough. "All right," he said, straining to keep his temper. "I listened to you, even though that's the biggest load of cow dung I've heard in all my years on this job. And I've listened to you—" he turned to Mrs. Vine "—telling me I'm heading for hellfire for accusing your son of murder. I don't want to hear any more from either of you. I'm the one wearing this badge and getting paid to do the police work in this town. So leave me alone and let me do it. I don't need hocus-pocus voodoo or Bible-waving fanatics to help me out. I'm going to nail this killer and stop his attacks. Is that quite clear?"

"At least warn those kids," Jeff asked him.

"I'll think about it," the sheriff said coldly. "There's enough fear and panic in this town without the likes of you fueling up more. You keep away from them, though. If I hear that you've been trying to spook them, I'll have you jailed for malicious mischief. Understand?"

Jeff nodded, flushing with embarrassment and rage. Derek couldn't help feeling a little sorry for the guy. The sheriff just dismissed his theories as if they were nothing.

Why? Then his eyes fell on the newspaper on the desk, and he began to see. The headlines ran: FOURTH MURDER —AND NO SUSPECTS. Under it was a slashing diatribe against the sheriff for not having arrested the killer yet. *He's under terrific·pressure*, Derek realized. The sheriff was getting hit from all sides to solve the cases. He must be getting worn down, and is just striking back at criticism. . . .

Mrs. Vine glared at Sheriff Adkins. "You're a hard-hearted man, Sheriff," she said. "I only pray that God doesn't have to break your heart for you to see the light."

"Out!" the sheriff yelled.

They left in a depressed group. Outside, Jeff shrugged. "Good luck, Derek," he said. "Let's hope that the sheriff really does know what he's doing."

Derek wasn't too certain of that. "Thanks for trying," he said. "I appreciate your faith in me. I really need it."

Mrs. Vine was still fuming. "Perhaps we should sing a hymn on the way home," she suggested. "To brighten our spirits."

"It's more likely to annoy the townsfolk," the pastor pointed out. "I think you'd be better off employing silent prayer."

"Nonsense," Mrs. Vine insisted. "These heathens could stand a little witnessing." She started out for home, loudly singing "Onward, Christian Soldiers."

Derek winced. His mother was always trying to convert people through intimidation. Some days he was beginning to think he might be better off in jail, after all. . . .

FOURTEEN

*LEO: Family members seem intent on causing problems.
Try talking things out with friends and relatives.*

Saturday morning found Robyn helping out in her
mother's store. Ray, the assistant, had taken the morning off, and Robyn had been asked to fill in, as she often
did. It wasn't that she minded working in the shop, just
that there were a million things she really wanted to get
done. Ah, well . . .

She was checking the shelves for anything that had
to be restocked from the back. The scents always made
her happy—spices, dried fruits and vegetables, the various rices in the food section. The incenses all had their
own heady aromas, too, which permeated the shop. And
there were plenty of her father's candles on display, each
with its own strong smell.

The food and incenses were down the left-hand wall
of the store as the customer walked in. On the right-

hand wall were the books, videos, New Age music CDs, and the area that she liked the best—the divination section. Tarot cards—over thirty different types— I Ching, the books on astrology, numerology, and color divination . . . these never tired her. Each time she came to the store, she checked out the latest arrivals.

The counter ran along the back of the store, a low glass display case with the register on it. In the case were the crystals, jewelry samples, and the small and large pyramids. There was so much to see and enjoy. Many of the regulars would browse for up to an hour, chatting when she or her mother was free.

Right now the shop was empty, and Mrs. Chantry had brewed them both cups of chamomile tea. As they sipped them, Mrs. Chantry fished out her favorite Tarot cards. These were quite battered by now, but she refused to retire them and get a new set. "I have a feel for these cards," she always said. Robyn rather liked the pictures —they were done in a sort of Art Nouveau style. The women all had long hair that curled around items in the pictures, and the men were all tall and thin, with soulful eyes.

As her mother idly played with the cards, Robyn finally brought herself to ask the question that had been nagging at her mind for days. "Mom, is everything all right with Dad?"

Her mother looked up. She didn't seem puzzled by the question—more like apprehensive. "What do you mean?"

"Well, the other day when I came home from school, he was upstairs, fast asleep. That's the third time in a

105

couple of weeks. And he seems so tired all the time. And preoccupied. Like there's something on his mind."

Mrs. Chantry let out a long breath. "Well," she admitted slowly. "I thought you'd notice, sooner or later." She shrugged. "Your father's been having some bad migraines recently. He used to have them years ago, but we thought they were gone. Only about six weeks ago, they started coming back. The only thing he can do is to lie down until they pass. You can't concentrate when one of those hits."

Robyn bit at her lower lip, worried. "Is he okay?"

"It's hard to say, sweetie." Robyn could see the strain in her mother's eyes, which she'd somehow managed not to notice before. "He's been going to the hospital for tests, but they don't seem to be able to find anything wrong. No brain tumor, or anything like that, thank God!"

It had never really struck her before, but with a shudder Robyn realized that her parents were mortal. They might suddenly do something really scary—like get sick, or even die. The thought of losing either of them shook her. But Mom had said there was nothing really wrong with Dad. . . . But they didn't know what was wrong, did they? How could they be sure? To cover the fact that her hands were shaking, Robyn put down her cup of tea and folded her hands in her lap. Her fingers kept twisting together, as if she was subconsciously trying to cross them for luck.

Mrs. Chantry sighed. "It's not a good time, is it, sweetie?" she asked, a thin smile on her face. "Those horrible murders, and now your father feeling bad. But he'll be all right. Believe me."

"I'll try," Robyn promised. Still, the haunting thoughts refused to go away.

"We all need a rest," her mother announced. "Maybe a short vacation or something. Spring break's coming up in a few weeks. Maybe I can get Ray to watch the shop, and we'll all take off for a while. That might be fun. To get away from Fremont for a bit, put its troubles behind us. Would you like that?"

"Yeah, it would be great," said Robyn, but she couldn't disguise the lack of enthusiasm in her voice.

Smiling, her mother touched Robyn's hand. "What's up? Got a new boyfriend you don't want to miss for a while?"

"No," replied Robyn, perhaps a shade too quickly. "I'm giving up on boys for now. Bryan sort of soured me on them."

Her mother started to lay out a pattern of cards on the countertop. "I told you he was wrong for you from the start. I don't know what it was that he did to upset you so much, and I'm not going to pry." She looked at Robyn, obviously hoping Robyn would volunteer the information. But for once Robyn didn't want to take her mother into her confidence. She'd have to own up to having been really stupid, and she couldn't bring herself to do that.

"But don't let him put you off all boys," her mother continued, when she realized that Robyn was doing her clam act. "There are plenty of nice ones out there." Her eyes narrowed. "What about that boy you've been seeing at school for this science project?"

"Jeff Goldstein?" Robyn shook her head emphatically. "He's not interested in me. And he's not really my type. He thinks astrology is garbage, and he's always putting me down." The last comment wasn't true, but she wanted to get her mother off the subject. Robyn wasn't certain how she felt about Jeff, but she didn't want her mother pressuring the two of them to get together.

"And Bryan Stockwell *was* your type?" Mrs. Chantry shot back. "Maybe you should start dating someone a bit different. It could broaden your horizons."

Right, thought Robyn. *Going out with him could be a date you'd never get over. Maybe he's a killer—though I don't really think so.* Aloud, she said: "I'm sure he's not interested in me, anyway. He's had plenty of chances to ask me out if he wants, but he never has."

"Hmm," her mother said. "Maybe he's just shy." Then, quietly, "I'm going to ask the cards about him."

"I don't believe in that stuff," Robyn said, rolling her eyes.

"Then what they say shouldn't affect you one way or the other." Her mother gathered the cards and shuffled them. After a moment's concentration, she laid them facedown on the counter and fanned them out. "Pick one."

Robyn stared down at the backs of the cards, suddenly nervous. "Mom, this is silly."

"Pick one," Mrs. Chantry repeated. When Robyn still didn't move, she added, "If you don't, I will."

"Oh, all right." Robyn stabbed out and lifted one of the cards. For the briefest second, she couldn't summon up the strength to turn it over. Then, almost defiantly, she slapped it down, faceup. "There." And she stopped in shock.

It was a man and a woman, entwined.

The Lovers.

She felt a cold shock run through her. Finally she managed to look up from the card into her mother's smug expression.

"I had a good feeling about this," Mrs. Chantry said.

"It's all nonsense," Robyn said heatedly. "I don't believe it for a minute."

"Now you're being silly. According to the cards, he's a perfect match for you. Why are you being so stubborn?" She suddenly peered over her daughter's shoulder, out the main window. "Looks like we're getting a customer." Then, with a puzzled frown, "Does this boy you're not interested in have glasses and dark hair?"

With a jolt, Robyn spun around to see Jeff staring at her through the window. She felt her face go red, and saw him flush as well. For a second, it looked like he was going to run away, but then he gathered his courage and came in the store.

"Uh, hi," he stammered nervously.

"Hello," said Mrs. Chantry brightly. "You must be Jeff Goldstein. I'm so pleased to meet you. I'm Robyn's mother." She held out her hand and Jeff shook it uncomfortably. Mrs. Chantry's eyes narrowed. "Haven't I seen you before?"

"Um, yes," Jeff admitted. "I've been in a few times."

"I thought you said that all of this New Age stuff was garbage," Robyn said. She was amazed at how cold her voice sounded.

Jeff blushed again. "Well, I told you I'd bought some of your father's candles," he said defensively. "Where did you think I'd gotten them?"

109

"I don't really care," Robyn said, furious at the smug expression on her mother's face. "If you'll excuse me, I really have to get back to work." She rose and went into the stockroom, refusing to look Jeff in the face. Once through the door, though, she stopped and listened.

"Don't take any notice of Robyn," her mother said. "She's in a mood today. So, you like my husband's work, then?"

"Very much," she heard Jeff reply. *Why won't he just leave?*

"Are you into all of the fantasy stuff? Tolkein and all that?"

"I kind of like it," Jeff admitted.

"How about coming along to an S.C.A. event?" asked Mrs. Chantry. "There's one coming up soon." Robyn almost died on the spot.

"Oh, Robyn told me about those."

"She did? Good. Well, the next one is a medieval banquet. I've got an extra ticket. Would you like to come along as our guest? You might enjoy it." Then— and Robyn could almost see the gleam in her mother's eye—she added, "Robyn will be there. She almost never misses them."

How could she do this? Robyn screamed silently. *Say no,* she prayed. *Please say no . . .*

"It sounds interesting," she heard Jeff reply. "Thank you. I'd like to come."

"Then that's settled." Robyn knew exactly who that remark was aimed at.

She closed her eyes, willing herself not to scream. She knew her face must be almost as red as her hair. She hardly heard the rest of Jeff's purchase of another candle, but sighed with relief when she heard the front door close behind him.

Then she shot out into the store and glared at her mother, furious. "How could you do that to me?" she cried.

Mrs. Chantry sniffed. "Well, someone had to do it, and you chickened out on me."

"I don't need your help to run my love life!"

"Don't be silly," her mother said. "I'm just helping you along a little bit, that's all. Anyway, maybe *you* don't need help, but that poor boy certainly does. He looked so lost when you left in a huff."

"That's because he's permanently lost," Robyn snapped. "Now call him up and tell him that the invitation's off. Make up anything, I don't care!"

"I'll do no such thing." Her mother started to lay out the cards again. "If you don't want him to come, then you tell him so. After all, you'll be seeing him at school. You can tell him there. But don't forget what the cards said. If you fight Fate, expect trouble."

FIFTEEN

CANCER: *A crisis today in your work. A bad day for decisions and meetings. Avoid conflicts.*

The watcher stood in the shadows at the rear of the Burger Barn. He hated this place and all it stood for—rampant consumerism, fast food, and bad taste. He suspected that the burgers were made from horseflesh or the bodies of all the rats that must die after eating the leftovers. He wished it was his mission to nuke every last one of these temples to a throwaway society. But, instead, he waited.

The spot he had selected was perfect. He knew that Ryan Sonderberg had to pass this way several times in the evening. Ryan, low boy in the ranks of the poorly paid after-school workers here, was the one given the task of constantly emptying the trash. Standing here, close to the huge dumpster, the watcher was in the best place to catch his victim. He was also in the perfect place to catch all of the stenches wafting from the trash.

Still, he had never expected his mission to be painless. Just right.

Steeling himself against the smell, he played with the murder weapon again. It was a small forklift, used to carry the pallets of supplies from the delivery trucks to the freezer in the store. He'd managed to slip it out when nobody had been looking, and had experimented with it. Two prongs stuck out the front, meant to be slotted into the gaps on the pallets and then lifted. Instead, as he had known, the prongs had a motor that could bring them together—very powerfully. Just like a crab snapping its claws.

The watcher smiled to himself. Now all he needed was for Ryan to come out when no one else was around . . .

It was one of those nights when it seemed like everyone in the world had decided to grab a burger and fries instead of cooking at home. Ryan was rushed off his feet, keeping the cooks supplied with the ingredients that they needed. The garbage grew in proportion, and—as always—Suzie Keller yelled for him to take it out.

Suzie was the manager of the place, and at the ripe old age of twenty-three, she seemed to think Ryan was there simply to be a slave. She enjoyed her feeling of power, and he really disliked her for it. But she *was* the boss, and he needed the money from this job to help out with college expenses next year. With a sigh and a mental picture of kicking Suzie a good one up the rear, he swung the can over his shoulder and kicked open the back door.

It was peaceful outside, the noises of the crowd indoors lost once the door closed behind him. He wished he could stay out awhile, just to catch his breath. But Suzie timed his runs, and if he was one second slower than she thought he should be, she screamed at him and threatened to dock his pay for laziness. As he headed for the dumpster, he realized that the small floodlight on the back of the building was out.

Typical! Probably Suzie's idea, to save money. Or of making his job a little more difficult. Well, he knew the route by heart now. He didn't really need the light. He was certainly too old to be scared of the dark. He found the dumpster as much by smell as by memory. What a job! He emptied the can and turned to go back in.

He heard the faint sound of the forklift starting up. Ryan peered into the gloom, then jumped as the twin prongs shot out from the shadows and slid past his ribs.

"What the hell?" he started to say, but he had time for no more. With a louder whine, the prongs moved together, their grip on him tightening. . . .

There were a few instants of terrible, crushing pain, and then nothing.

The watcher examined his handiwork. Ryan's body hung supported from the forklift, the chest a mass of blood and broken bones, impossibly thin. Crushed in the claw of a giant crab. Perfect.

He took the first picture, then moved slightly to take the second. Just as the flash went off, the back door opened and a strident voice yelled:

"Get your butt in here, Sonderberg!"

The killer whirled. The second time he'd almost been seen! Like the last time, he triggered the flash on his camera into the face of the person in the doorway, then turned and ran.

Suzie Keller staggered, blinded by the flash in her eyes. The floodlight for the waste area was out, too. "If this is some dumb trick," she snarled, "I'm gonna have your job for it." She heard footsteps running away— Sonderberg? Then her outflung hand touched something warm, wet, and sticky.

The garbage! He'd tricked her into walking into the garbage, to make her look like a total jerk! She'd murder that little creep!

Then, as her vision slowly cleared, she discovered that she was slightly too late to murder him. The sticky warmth all over her hand was his dripping blood.

She screamed, loud and long, and then fainted.

SIXTEEN

LEO: Suspicions and fears haunt you today. Go with your heart, but don't neglect your mind. Avoid arguments with friends.

Robyn carefully replaced the bishop of the candle chess set in its box and beamed at her father. He seemed to have been much better these last few days. No headaches. Maybe he was coming out of whatever it was again. "It's really lovely," she told him. "You're excelling yourself."

"We aim to please," He said with a laugh. "Think John and Fern will like them?"

"They'll love them. Will you have them done in time?"

"Sure." He nodded toward his cupboards. "I've put that Vlad thing on hold for now. It really bothers me, dealing with figures of death. Give me something with life in it any day!"

Robyn smiled. "You're so full of it yourself."

"You seem pretty chipper these days, too." Her father made as if to ruffle her hair with his wax-encrusted hands. Robyn gave a mock scream and jumped back. "This new boyfriend of yours seems to be good for you."

"He's *not* my boyfriend," Robyn answered. "It wasn't my idea to invite him to the S.C.A. event. It was Mom's."

"Well, I hope he's not *her* new boyfriend, then." He chuckled. "She said that you two just need a little nudge in the right direction. She's a smart woman, your mother."

"Not in this case," replied Robyn. "Jeff and I are just partners in the science fair. Nothing more—and we don't want to be."

"Are you sure that's what he thinks? He accepted that invitation fast enough when your mother told him you'd be there." He looked at her perceptively.

"That's silly," she said, trying to sound convincing. "Anyway, have a good day. I'll see you after school."

"What's the rush? Your mother hasn't even honked the horn yet."

She said quietly, "I just want to catch the news first."

His good humor evaporated and he nodded. "Yeah. It's still pretty scary for you kids, isn't it? Take care, honey."

In the kitchen, Robyn turned on the portable TV and tuned in to the local channel. It had become something of a morning ritual with her, since Natalie's death almost two weeks earlier. Though there had been no further killings, she knew it was just a matter of—

"—horrible," the distraught-looking blond woman in

117

a Burger Barn outfit was saying. "He was dead, and just hanging there."

The reporter's face came on. "So, there we have it," she said, almost maliciously. "Another young man has become the fourth victim of the Teen Terror."

Oh, God! Robyn thought, her heart freezing. Terrified, wondering which of her friends was dead this time, she stood spellbound in front of the set.

A picture of Ryan Sonderberg flashed onto the screen. The reporter's voice-over continued: "At about eight-thirty last night, the murder victim was discovered by the manager of the Burger Barn on Howell's Road where he worked. Young Ryan Sonderberg had been crushed in the viselike grip of a forklift truck. The manager, Suzanne Keller, narrowly missed seeing the killer, but she did manage to tell police that the murderer was apparently taking photographs of the body. I spoke again with Sheriff Adkins."

A small message, RECORDED EARLIER, flashed on the screen. Sheriff Adkins's large stomach appeared, the man himself in tow.

"Sheriff," the reporter asked, "is this the first time that a report has been made of pictures of the body being taken?"

For a second, it looked as if the sheriff was about to punch the woman, then he thought better of it. "No," he admitted. "The father of the last victim reported the same thing. We consider it likely that the killer is photographing the bodies of all of his victims."

"Why do you think he's doing that?"

He shot her a filthy look. "Because he's *sick*, you numbskull. He gets his kicks from murdering kids, and then takes pictures so he can get his jollies again later. Now, let me be. I'm busy."

The picture changed back to the news anchor at the studio. Robyn clicked off the TV and stood there, frozen in shock.

The phone rang and she scooped it up quickly. "Jeff?" *Why had she assumed it would be him?*

"Yeah," his voice said. "I guess you just saw the news, then."

"Yes," she admitted quietly. "Ryan Sonderberg." She'd never been that close to him, but she still grieved. For him, for his family, and for the fact that they had expected something like this and had been unable to prevent it. "Look, I'll talk to you at school, okay?"

"Sure."

She ran outside just in time to catch her mother unlocking the van's doors. Her mother looked very surprised. "Aren't you waiting for the sound of the horn anymore?"

"There's been another murder," Robyn told her. "Another kid from my class."

Mrs. Chantry went white. "Oh, God," she said, almost in a whisper. Then, angrily, "And the police still haven't caught the maniac that's doing it?" Robyn shook her head. Suddenly her mother grabbed Robyn and hugged her tightly. "It's a nightmare," she said. "I'm so scared for you. And Debi, and Jeff, and all of your friends. When's it ever going to end?"

"Maybe soon," Robyn said. "Jeff and I have a theory. The sheriff has to listen to us now."

On the way to pick up Debi, Robyn explained what they had deduced so far. Mrs. Chantry sat silently through it all. Finally, she asked, "And the sheriff wouldn't listen to Jeff?"

"No. He said that it was just a silly fantasy, and threw him out."

"And this Ryan was on the list you'd given him?"

"Uh huh."

Her mother looked grim. "Can you work up another list? Who might be next? And give it to me this time. I'll get a few people together and tell them what you two have figured out. I guarantee you, the sheriff will listen this time. Or he will if he ever expects to get re-elected."

"Well," Robyn said slowly, afraid of what was going to happen, "we do know a few things. Here's Debi's place. Pull in." Once her mother had the car off the road and had honked the horn, Robyn added, "It'll be a female born in the sign of Leo."

Mrs. Chantry paled. *"You're* a Leo."

"Don't I know it." And, Robyn privately admitted, she was terrified. If the killer *was* Derek Vine, she'd offended him enough times to be considered a very likely victim of choice . . .

As Debi and Robyn approached the school building, Dana joined them. She'd been very subdued since Natalie's murder, and she'd clearly heard the latest news, too. Entering the building, Debi realized that the old sounds of laughter and inane chatter were virtually dead. The students had hardly been in a frame of mind to endure school lately, let alone enjoy it. It was like walking into a cemetery—where all of the other mourners wondered

120

who would be the next to die, and which of their fellows was killing them.

As they headed for their lockers, they passed Derek. He waved a copy of the school paper in their direction. "You've done it again, haven't you, Jean Stephenson?" he said coldly.

Robyn had had enough. She turned to face him. "I've done *what* again?"

"So you are the mysterious Stephenson, eh?" he mused. He looked pleased with the trick he had played to get her to admit to it. "It figures. Don't you read your own predictions?"

"Get to the point."

"Yesterday's forecast for Cancer was a bad day—and Ryan was a Cancer. He told me just yesterday morning."

"Listen, Derek," Robyn snarled, "I just read the stars —I don't make their predictions come true. You're barking up the wrong tree."

"Sure," he agreed. "And it's just a coincidence that you predicted all of the deaths, right?"

Debi grabbed Robyn's arm. "Forget it," she advised. "You won't get anywhere with him. My mom says that you should never argue with an idiot; people might not be able to tell you apart."

"Uh oh," Dana said, looking down toward the school entrance. "Guys . . ."

They followed her gaze and saw Sheriff Adkins with two of his deputies striding toward them. His face was cold. He pointed straight at Derek. "Get him," he told his deputies.

Derek looked stunned. He looked at the two deputies in bewilderment. "What are you doing?"

"Derek Vine, you're under arrest." The sheriff glared at him. "We've got eyewitnesses that place you close to the Burger Barn at the time of the murder last night."

Robyn was almost as shocked as Derek. Dana and Debi looked equally astonished. Robyn had always wondered in the back of her mind if maybe it *was* Derek who was killing people. . . . But for this to happen, right in front of their eyes!

Sheriff Adkins glanced at them, then told his first deputy, "Read him his rights, then take him off and book him." To the three girls he said, "Get lost."

For once, none of them took offense. They shot down the corridor to their lockers in silence. Only when they were there did they stop and stare at one another. Robyn was too shaken even to speak. She leaned against the lockers to stay upright. If she didn't, she was afraid she'd faint.

Derek—guilty! And arrested . . . at last, it was all over.

"What's with you three?" asked Joe, coming to join them.

"The police just arrested Derek Vine," Dana said in a hollow voice. "He's the Teen Terror."

Joe went almost white. "You're kidding!"

"No, she isn't," said Sheriff Adkins, striding over. "Butler, which is Vine's locker?"

Gesturing, Joe glared at the sheriff. "This one. Why?"

"Open it."

"Now, wait a minute," Joe told him. "That's his property. Don't you have to have a search warrant or something?"

"Well, look at the amateur lawyer." The sheriff pulled

122

a piece of paper from his pocket. "Guess what this is? I don't conduct illegal searches for lawyers to toss my cases out of court."

Joe glanced at the warrant uncertainly. Then, with a shrug, he used his master keys. After a moment, the locker door opened. Sheriff Adkins pushed him aside, then started to root in the locker. He looked down at the girls. "Didn't I tell you to get lost?"

"We have to get our books from our own lockers," Robyn retorted.

"Well, then, just—" He stopped and a wide smile crossed his face. Dragging out a history textbook, he held it open. There were several photos in it. "Well, look at what we've got here."

Robyn could just barely see that the top one was a picture of Jenny Warren, lying on the ground, a scarf around her neck. A wave of nausea passed over her. A picture of Jenny's murdered body . . . in Derek's locker . . .

"I think that this is all we need now," Sheriff Adkins said with satisfaction. "We've got him hog-tied for sure." He turned and walked off.

Shaking, Joe shut the locker door again. "I don't believe it," he said quietly. "I mean—who'd have believed that the Vine kid was guilty?"

"I *don't* believe it," Debi said firmly.

Puzzled, Robyn looked at her friend. "But you just saw—"

"Come on, Robyn!" Debi cried. "It's the oldest game in the book. Those photos could have been put there by anybody. There are no negatives. And why would Derek

123

be dumb enough to keep pictures like that in his locker?"

"Besides that," Dana added softly, "he doesn't take that history course."

Robyn's mind was almost reeling now. "You mean he was framed? But he was seen at the murder site. . . ."

"It was a Burger Barn!" Debi said angrily. "For God's sake, half the school eats there!"

"But . . ." Joe looked from one girl to another, his face a mass of confusion. "Who'd want to frame him?"

Debi looked at Robyn meaningfully. "My vote goes for the one person who could have done this. The one person we know who had access to the student records. And who happens to have a very nice, expensive camera in his room."

Robyn realized what Debi was getting at. "No!" she yelled. "Not Jeff! It can't be Jeff!" Even as she said it, she wondered why she felt so sure. What did she really know about him, and what he might or might not do?

"Wake up," Debi told her. "I know you like him, but he's the only person who it could have been."

Shaking, Robyn looked at her friend and read only utter conviction there. But it *couldn't* possibly be Jeff.

SEVENTEEN

AQUARIUS: Friends can cause trouble today, but it's possible to work things out. Avoid conflicts of interest.

The news of Derek's arrest spread through the school faster than anyone would have thought possible. With the arrest, it seemed as though the black clouds in the students' spirits had finally been lifted. Except, Debi reflected, for herself, Robyn, and Dana.

They were all utterly convinced that the wrong person had been arrested for the crimes.

Robyn refused to believe that Jeff could be guilty, but that was stubbornness, not logic, at work. Debi had seen her friend being slowly drawn to that weird loner, even if she kept denying it. Why else was she so adamant in refusing to believe that Jeff was a likely suspect? Debi couldn't see who else it could possibly be. Dana didn't believe it was either one of them, but she had no ready answers.

They were in the small office devoted to the school newspaper, getting ready for the next weekly issue. At least, that was the theory. In fact, all three girls were simply sitting there, lost in their own thoughts. Ms. Tepper, the teacher who worked with them on the paper, had stopped by earlier to check on progress, but then she had left them to it.

"Okay," Robyn said, breaking the silence. "We know that Jeff could have gotten the information out of the school system. *Could have*," she stressed, looking at Debi significantly. "But there have to be other people who could have done it."

"Okay," agreed Dana. "Let's think. There's Miss Mallinson, the secretary. She puts the information in, so she could have taken it out."

"But the killer is male," Debi objected. "The manager at the Burger Barn caught a glimpse of him. And so did Natalie's dad. Mallinson's out."

"She could have given the information to the killer," Dana suggested.

"Right." Debi sighed theatrically. "So we not only have a killer, but a school secretary who supplies him with information. It's a bit farfetched."

"I agree," Robyn said. "What about Principal Berger?"

"No," Dana said. "He can't work a pencil sharpener, let alone the school computer. He has Miss Mallinson get him printouts of what he needs. I've heard him ask her."

"I don't know of any other kid who knows enough about computers to break into the system," Debi pointed out. "Which just leaves Jeff."

"No," objected Robyn. "There's one other person—Mr. Traynor. *He* could have done it."

Debi considered this. The idea that a teacher might be the murderer had never occurred to her. And Traynor was the science teacher. He must have the computer skills to break into the files.

"And he doesn't like Derek Vine at all," Dana said softly. "He's a rabid atheist and hates everyone from Derek's church. I heard him say so to Ms. Tepper. And he's always making fun of my being a Baptist."

Debi found the implication somewhat scary. A teacher might be killing students. . . . She shuddered. Not that she liked all of the teachers. And she certainly didn't like Old Twinkletoes. But could she picture him *killing* anyone?

"But how do we find out if he *is* the one?" asked Robyn. "I mean, we can't ask him for an alibi for all the murders, can we?"

"It's not our job," protested Debi. "All we have to do is tell the sheriff our suspicions. He's bound to have to follow them up."

"He didn't follow up what Jeff told him," said Robyn.

"*If* Jeff really told him," argued Debi. "Or maybe Jeff was deliberately unconvincing, so the sheriff wouldn't suspect him?"

"I don't think so," Robyn protested weakly. "But I think we'd need to have some solid clue before we could accuse Mr. Traynor. I'll bet the sheriff's had all kinds of crank calls already, accusing half the people in town."

That left them in silence for a while. Then Dana snapped her fingers. "You know, we're going about this the wrong way."

127

"What do you mean?" asked Debi, puzzled.

"Well, we're assuming that whoever the killer is gets his victim's information from the school computer."

"So?"

"Aren't there any *written* records that he could use instead?"

Debi thought about that for a while. "I know there used to be," she agreed. "But they were all transferred to the computer about three or four years ago, I think."

"So what happened to all the paper files?" Dana asked triumphantly. "Maybe the killer is using them?"

"Joe would know," Debi said slowly. "He's been here long enough. I'll go and ask him."

She left the room and headed for Joe's basement "office." It was actually just an old storage room that he'd taken over and put a chair and table in for when he had a break. He also posted notes on the door as to where he could be found when he was working. Luckily, he was just coming up the stairs when she arrived.

"What's the rush?" he asked her.

"I was looking for you, Joe."

He grinned. "Must be my lucky day. Not many pretty girls come hunting for me. What can I do for you?"

"Do you remember when the school records were all transferred to computer a couple of years back?" When he nodded, she asked, "What happened to all the paper files?"

"Principal Berger gave them to me to burn," Joe said. "I just tossed them in the furnace."

Feeling deflated, Debi thanked him and headed back to her friends. "No good," she said glumly. "Joe burned them all years ago."

"So we're back to the computer again," said Dana. "And Jeff and Traynor."

"It's not Jeff," said Robyn tiredly. "So let's not go into that again."

"Okay," Dana said. "Then let's try another approach. Is there any connection between the times of the murders?"

"Well," Debi said, "they all took place at night. Between about eight and ten o'clock."

"That's because it's dark then, and the killer won't be seen," Robyn suggested.

"And how about the timing?" Dana asked, scribbling on a sheet of paper. "There was exactly a week between the first two killings. And then—" Her voice caught for a moment, but she pressed on. "Natalie was murdered thirteen days later."

"And Ryan last night," finished Debi. "Another eleven days."

"Seven . . . thirteen . . . eleven . . ." Shaking her head, Dana admitted, "I can't see any connection."

"Maybe there isn't any," Debi said. "Maybe he just kills people when he feels like it."

"No," said Robyn slowly. "No, he's using an astrological key . . ." She snapped her fingers. "Derek!"

"Now you think he did it?" Debi objected.

"No—I mean he gave me the answer! I know what triggered the murders!" Robyn grabbed the stack of back issues. "He said *I'd* predicted the murders in my horoscopes, but I think it's the other way around. I think the killer reads my column and uses it to decide when he'll kill someone." She had found the first entry, Aries, for the day Jenny was killed. "A bad day," she whispered.

"And I'll bet the first time this year that I wrote that Taurus would have a bad day was when Alan was killed."

It took them less than two minutes to confirm her idea. Each death had in fact taken place the day after her column predicted a bad day for the sign. Debi looked at Robyn. "So, where does that get us? Anybody could be reading these things."

"Don't you see?" Robyn was excited. "Now that we know what sets off the murders, we can prevent another one very simply. Logically, the next murder would be of a Leo girl. All we have to do is make certain that I don't predict a bad day for Leo."

"Brilliant," agreed Debi. "So even if we can't figure out who the killer is yet, we can stop him from striking again."

"Didn't you just turn in another column?" asked Dana. "The paper's going to press tomorrow, remember?"

"Right!" Robyn dashed over to the finished file and looked through it for her column. It covered the next week starting the following Monday. "Here it is." She skimmed down it, then froze. "Oh, God—next Tuesday." She held out the paper.

"Change it," Debi ordered. "Now."

Nodding, Robyn crossed out that entry. She slipped the paper into the typewriter, and after a few seconds to think, she typed furiously. When she was done, she read it out: "A day for dreams to come true. Think positive, and good things may happen."

"Much better," Debi agreed. "That should fix it."

"Meanwhile," Dana added, "maybe you'd better steer clear of Jeff. Just in case."

Jeff! Robyn slapped her head. "I forgot—I promised to meet him this morning. All this stuff about Derek and the horoscopes put it clean out of my mind. And I didn't see him all day. What must he think?"

Dana grabbed Robyn's arms and shook her. "Isn't anything we're saying getting through to you? Jeff's a prime suspect for the Teen Terror! Stop worrying about hurting his feelings, and start worrying about staying alive."

Pulling herself free, Robyn shook her head. "It's not that easy. My mom invited him to go to the S.C.A. meeting on Saturday with us."

Dana and Debi exchanged glances. The fear they felt showed clearly in their faces. But Debi could see that Robyn was finally starting to consider the possibility that they were right. "Maybe that'll be okay," she said to Robyn. "He's not likely to do anything around all those people. Just stick with your folks and don't let him get you alone."

"Besides," Dana added, "if he is the killer, he probably won't strike until Tuesday." She tapped the sheet of paper that Robyn still held. "And now that you've made those changes, maybe not even then."

"Uh huh," said Robyn in a hollow voice. "We're perfectly safe now—aren't we?"

EIGHTEEN

LEO: *Avoid bad advice from well-meaning friends. Follow your instincts, but be careful when making decisions.*

By Friday morning, the knot of uncertainty in Robyn's stomach had grown to almost overwhelming proportions. She clicked on the TV news as she finished her morning herb tea. Had anything happened? Was she wrong about Derek? Were they safe now that he was in jail?

Could the killer really be Jeff?

As the news anchor led the viewers through the various stories, Robyn's mind drifted. The idea of Jeff being the killer seemed absurd to her. He'd always been perfectly nice, even thoughtful and caring. Not only to her, but to everyone she'd ever seen him with. Except when he got embarrassed. Then he just seemed to run and hide—either physically or inside his head. He'd probably had long experience with dealing with insults. But he seemed to be the last person in the world who would ever want to hurt anyone.

And, she had to admit, despite herself, she was beginning to see beneath the outer awkwardness. He was bright and eager to please. And if you really looked at him, you realized he could sort of be good-looking. He actually had very pretty eyes. And his hair was thick and shiny. Was it as soft as it looked? Robyn shook her head suddenly, ending these pointless thoughts.

But—if Jeff was the Teen Terror? Then what?

She was torn, and there didn't seem to be an answer to it.

She abruptly blinked back her attention to the TV. A picture of Derek's mother was on it. She was being interviewed outside the sheriff's office. The newswoman was asking: "—your son guilty?"

"No, he isn't," Mrs. Vine said firmly. "He's a good, God-fearing boy, and I am quite confident that God will vindicate him."

"Then why do you think he's under arrest?"

"As a scapegoat," Mrs. Vine replied. "Sheriff Adkins has been pressured to make an arrest, and he simply picked my son as the target for his vile accusations. And, as soon as Derek is exonerated, I aim to sue the sheriff and the town for false arrest and imprisonment."

The van's horn honked outside and Robyn switched off the TV with a sigh. Despite her aversion to Derek's mother, there was probably some truth in what she had said. The sheriff had needed to make an arrest, and whoever the real killer was had certainly framed Derek pretty effectively.

Blowing a kiss to her father, Robyn dashed outside

133

and into the van. With an expensive-sounding grinding of gears, Mrs. Chantry swerved out into the street. She slapped the horn, warning the truck she'd cut off to stay out of her way. The driver's response was one-fingered. Robyn shuddered.

"You're very quiet this morning," her mother said.

"That's because I'm praying we get to school alive," replied Robyn dryly.

"Everyone's a critic." Mrs. Chantry smiled at her daughter. "How's Jeff?"

"I don't know," Robyn answered, perhaps a little too emphatically. "I haven't seen him for a couple days."

Her mother looked questioningly at her until Robyn pointed back at the road. "You two didn't argue, did you?"

How could Robyn explain this? "No, Mom. I haven't really talked to him. But . . ." Screwing up her courage, she plunged on, "I'm pretty sure that Derek Vine isn't the Teen Terror. Debi and Dana think Jeff probably is."

"That nice boy?" Mrs. Chantry asked, astonished. "Nonsense!"

"Mom, you don't really know him too well. You're too trusting."

"The cards like him."

Robyn sighed theatrically. "Mom, the cards just say what you want them to. It's just wishful thinking. You want me happily dating, and the whole thing."

"I always want what's best for you," her mother replied. "But the cards never lie. You mark my words, this suspicion about Jeff Goldman is completely unfounded."

"*Goldstein,*" Robyn corrected her.

"Whatever. Anyway, you shouldn't listen too seriously to these friends of yours. None of them know any more about life than you do, and some of them a great deal less. They're probably just jealous that you've hooked Jeff and they haven't."

"I doubt that's it," Robyn said dryly. "He's not considered exactly a catch, you know."

"Then they're very shallow. He seems like a very good bargain to me." Her mother eyed her again, until Robyn's choked scream made her focus back on traffic. "I notice that you didn't say that *you* thought he was this killer."

"That's because I don't know what to think," Robyn said miserably. "I can't make my mind up about him at all. I know he seems to like me—every now and then his defenses sort of drop and he lets a bit out. But he doesn't seem able to do anything about it. And I don't know if I'd really like it if he did."

Her mother snorted. "Honestly, you teenagers today think you invented uncertainty! Robyn, Jeff's probably scared you'll turn him down. I think he's shown a lot of bravery already. He visited you in the shop, and you almost slapped his face."

Robyn cringed. "Mom, he was just shopping. He didn't know I'd be there."

"Right! He was dancing around uncertainly on the sidewalk for ages before he came in. And he bought the first candle I offered him. Believe me, it was you he was after, not shopping."

"Then why doesn't he say anything?"

"Haven't you been listening to me? He already has. He's a very shy boy, obviously, and it's not easy for him to express himself. I think it's about time that you made up your mind. Do you want to encourage him or not? The next step has to be up to you. He'll need a little help." She grinned. "How do you think I caught your father? He'd never have asked me out if I hadn't almost dragged him along."

"Parents!"

They pulled into the Smolinske driveway and Mrs. Chantry honked her horn. Debi came dashing out, an excited look on her face. Jumping in, she said, "Publication day today!"

Robyn had almost forgotten about that. "Oh, right!" The changed predictions—and maybe the first move in stopping the hidden killer.

Debi and Robyn were barely out of Mrs. Chantry's van when Dana rushed over, pale and waving a copy of the newly-printed paper.

"It's changed," she said, panic in her voice. "The horoscope. It's been changed."

Robyn grabbed the paper and looked at it. For Tuesday's prediction in Leo, it now read: "Your worst nightmares come true. Positive thinking won't help here." Robyn went cold. "That's not even what I wrote the first time around," she said softly.

"The killer must have changed it," Dana said. "It means that he knew you'd altered it somehow."

The three of them looked at one another. The killer must have been watching them, somehow, or known about the switch. . . . Debi looked at Robyn. "Did you tell anyone about the change?"

"No," Robyn said, thinking hard. "Just the three of us knew."

"You didn't happen to mention this to Jeff, did you?" asked Debi.

"No!" Robyn was angry and hurt at the implication. "I haven't talked to him for days."

"We can soon settle this," Dana broke in. "All we have to do is to check the original columns that went in to the printers. They always return them with the new papers. Maybe whoever changed the column did it by hand."

"That's a long shot," Robyn said. "But it's worth a try. Come on!" She led the way to the newspaper room, feeling very tense and nervous. Why was she so scared about what they might find?

In the room, there was no sign of the documents they wanted. After a fruitless search, Dana said, "Maybe they've already been thrown away?"

"We could check with Ms. Tepper," suggested Robyn. "She might have them for some reason."

They went along to the staff room. Outside the door Debi and Dana looked at Robyn, and she nervously knocked on the door. It was opened by Mr. Traynor, who blinked at them all, as if astounded to see students in school. Robyn asked for the English teacher, and he vanished again. After a moment, Ms. Tepper came out, closing the door firmly behind her.

Robyn's feelings about Ms. Tepper were decidedly mixed. She was a good enough teacher, but her personality left a lot to be desired. She insisted on being Miz Tepper. "I'm not shackled by my marital status," she snapped. The students read this to mean: *I'm divorced*, but that was just a rumor. Most of the students could never believe she'd ever been married.

She was tall, a shade under six feet, and her dark hair was cropped close to her head. She had very little shape, and the clothing she wore tended to simply hang there.

With a sudden shock, Robyn realized: *In the dark, in a coat, she could be taken for a man*.

"What is it?" Ms. Tepper snapped. "I haven't got all day to stand around gossiping, you know."

"Er . . . it's the newspaper, Ms. Tepper," Robyn said, trying to ignore the crawling of her skin. "Somebody changed what I wrote."

"That's what an editor does," the teacher said. "Though, God knows, we're not appreciated for it. You writers think that every word that drips from your pen is made of gold."

"But, one of my predictions," Robyn said. She held up the paper.

Ms. Tepper sniffed. "You know my opinions about them," she said. "If it wasn't popular, I'd have excised the column years ago. I certainly didn't change any silly predictions you may have made. I just clean up your atrocious grammar."

"Oh." Robyn looked at her friends.

"Do you still have the original copies?" asked Debi.

"Why? For posterity?" Ms. Tepper raised her eyes to the skies. "So you can one day be compared to Hemingway and called a national treasure? I threw them out once the paper was printed." With a curt nod, she returned to the staff room and her coffee.

"Maybe Joe still has them, then?" suggested Robyn. In unspoken agreement, the three of them headed for the basement.

Joe was there, stoking up the furnace with burnable

138

trash. He gave them a grin when they arrived and listened as they explained their quest. Then he shrugged. "I emptied the trash last night," he told them. "Most of the paper has gone into the furnace, but there's some I haven't burned yet." He pointed to a can that was about half full. "Maybe you'll be lucky, and it's in there. Otherwise it's burned, I'm afraid."

With sinking hearts they searched the can, but what they had feared was true: there was no sign of the original sheet of astrology predictions. Joe had unwittingly burned it.

Back upstairs, they headed for their first class, deep in depression. Robyn was especially down, knowing that Debi and probably Dana still suspected that Jeff was the person behind this. She didn't want to believe it. But there was just that little nagging doubt in the back of her mind that maybe her friends were right, and Jeff wasn't the person he seemed to be.

Could she be so wrong about him?

And what about her new suspicions? "Another possibility just came to me," she said slowly. "Maybe the killer is Ms. Tepper?"

"What?" Debi looked at her as if she was crazy.

"Well, she could pass for a man in bad light," Robyn plunged on. "And she could have changed the prediction. She must have seen it, and she might have seen the original if she'd checked the column earlier that day. And she had the originals burned much earlier than normal."

Dana looked uncertain. "I don't know," she said with a sigh. "I mean, I know she's a bit weird . . . But—a murderer?"

"She doesn't seem to like her students very much," added Robyn. "And she has—had—all of the victims in her classes. Also Derek Vine."

"I think you're reaching a bit," Debi said. "Does she have any computer skills? Could she have access to the school records?"

They were silent. Robyn simply didn't know, and neither did the others. "There are too many unknowns," Robyn said.

"We have to talk to the sheriff again," Debi said firmly. "I know everyone thinks that the murders will stop while Derek's behind bars, but we know better."

"It's not likely to do much good." Robyn sighed. "Even my mom is convinced that it's all over, and she was ready to take on the sheriff hand-to-hand less than a week ago."

"But we can't just do nothing," Dana pointed out.

"And if it *is* Jeff," Debi said, with a long, hard look at Robyn, "don't say anything to him. You'll have to act like everything's fine."

"Terrific," Robyn muttered. "I feel like you're asking me to betray him."

"If he's guilty, then he's the one doing the betraying," replied Debi. "And if he isn't, you can always apologize later. Anyway, you'll be perfectly safe with him until Tuesday." She shrugged. "If he likes you as much as he seems to, he's probably picked some other Leo girl for his next victim."

"Not necessarily," objected Debi. "Maybe he's obsessed with Robyn. Maybe it's because he's picked her? You know, like those deranged fans who attack actors they think they're in love with?"

"Or maybe he just *likes* me?" Robyn countered sarcastically. "My mom is certain he's just shy, and that he's really a great guy."

"What about you?" asked Dana.

What about *me*?

On their way home, Robyn and Debi stopped in at the sheriff's office. Feeling foolish and very insecure, Robyn asked the deputy on duty if she could speak with Sheriff Adkins. In moments, they were ushered into the back office. The sheriff looked up from his cluttered desk.

"You can have a couple of minutes," he told them, "but you must realize that my time's taken up preparing the stuff for the grand jury." He waved them to seats. "So, what can I do for you young ladies?"

"We think that you've arrested the wrong person," Robyn said, as meekly as she could. Despite this, the sheriff gave her a withering glare and leaned forward.

"I think we can convict him with what we've got." He sounded pretty mad.

"I'm sure you can," Debi agreed. "But doesn't some of it look fishy to you? I mean, who in his right mind would keep proof they were a killer in his school locker?"

"He couldn't very well keep it at home," Sheriff Adkins argued. "And he isn't in his right mind. Besides, a lot of these flaky killers really want to get caught. It's attention that they're really after, not killing people as such."

"Did Derek confess to any of the killings?" asked Robyn.

Scowling, the sheriff said, "No. He doesn't seem to

141

understand we can already nail him good with this. He's been sitting in his cell, reading the Bible. I think he's trying to make it look good for himself, is all. Won't work."

"Maybe he's reading the Bible because he's a Christian," Debi pointed out.

"Look, let's cut to the chase," the sheriff said. "Is this all you came in here for?"

"No." Robyn explained their theory about the killings being tied to her predictions in the school paper, and then handed over a copy of the changed column. The sheriff sighed again.

"Look, kids," he said, striving to sound patient and failing. "There could be any number of other things that sparked Vine off. It didn't have to be your column."

"But it can't have been Derek," objected Debi. "He was already in jail when the paper was changed."

"Anybody could have changed it, for any number of reasons. I'm sure I got the right person."

Robyn had suspected that he wouldn't listen, but he was being so stubborn. "And you were sure when Jeff Goldstein brought you the list of possible victims that there wasn't anything to that, either. But Ryan Sonderberg was killed. What will it take to convince you that we're right? Another murder?"

The sheriff stared at her coldly. "If there is another one, I'll be the first to admit that Vine isn't guilty. But he is guilty, so there won't be. Now, off you go. I got work to do."

Robyn stood up. "You'll have much more work to do on Tuesday," she said. "Because if you don't listen to us, there will be another murder."

"Out."

In the street, Debi glared back at the building. "What a jackass." She snorted.

"Well, we knew he probably wouldn't listen," Robyn reminded her. "He wouldn't have arrested Derek if he didn't really believe him to be guilty. And one changed entry in the school newspaper just isn't enough to shake his faith. We'd have to get a lot more proof to convince him."

"I just wish there was some better way to find out who the killer really is."

"It's not Jeff," Robyn said quickly. "I'm certain of that."

"I just hope you're right," Debi said. "Because if you're wrong, you may wind up *dead* wrong."

NINETEEN

LEO: Enjoy yourself. Be sociable. Good things may come of the weekend.

As she got ready for the S.C.A. evening, Robyn thought, as always, about the recent murders. The tension in town seemed to have evaporated now that a suspect was behind bars—many people were convinced that Derek was guilty before he'd even been tried, let alone convicted. Robyn was convinced it was partly because he wasn't that popular, and partly because people desperately wanted to believe the nightmare was over.

Robyn changed slowly into her outfit for the night. It was her turn to be one of the serving girls at the feast, and they were always expected to be rather saucy. She wore a low-cut top and a long skirt, both in light green. They offset her red hair well, and when she donned her leather sandals, she certainly looked the part of a medieval barmaid. She hoped she wasn't showing *too* much cleavage, though. . . . She didn't want to give Jeff the wrong idea about these events!

Jeff was borrowing a costume from her father, since he didn't have anything appropriate of his own. Mr. Chantry had decided to dress him as a traveling merchant, in a long cloak, tunic, and tights. Despite her worries, when Robyn saw him, she couldn't help smiling. Jeff looked pretty good in his costume, actually, but he seemed so embarrassed she had to laugh.

"Nice legs," she told him, admiring how they looked in his red tights. His face was close to the same shade.

"Nice . . . earrings," he replied, looking considerably below the level of her ears.

She glanced down. "It's too much, isn't it?" she sighed. "I thought so."

"Oh, I'm not complaining!" he said hastily.

"I'll bet you're not," said Mrs. Chantry, breezing into the room. She had worn her usual outfit, that of a gypsy fortune-teller. She had on a long skirt with an intricate woven pattern, and a low-cut blouse of her own. Both wrists had golden bracelets with dangling charms, and she had a golden band around her forehead, pinning her own rather wild hair in place. She looked, Robyn had to admit, very fetching. Now Mrs. Chantry examined her daughter and Jeff. "Well, I think you make a fine couple."

Robyn gritted her teeth. Mom was matchmaking again. . . . Was she going to have to put up with this for the whole evening? How would Jeff take it? Would he think *she* had put her mother up to this? Would Mrs. Chantry's aggression terrify him?

Then she had to remind herself that the very fact he

was here at all was because of her mother. After all, this wasn't exactly a date. He was—theoretically—attending as a friend of the family, not as her boyfriend, or anything. Which was good. Wasn't it?

"Come on," her father said, standing in the doorway. He had changed into his own blacksmith costume, and had his bag of tools in his hand. "Time to hitch the horses to the wagon and be off."

Robyn smiled at Jeff's vaguely alarmed expression. "We're taking the van," she explained. "But for the whole evening, it's more fun if we call everything by medieval terms."

The meeting was being held in the Baptist Church hall and was attended by people from miles around. They were all in costumes, some very elaborate. There were gypsy dancing girls, knights in fine costumes (since it was a feast and not a battle, there was no armor worn). There were merchants, who were selling real-enough wares at tables in the halls—from crystals and tarot-card sets to forged metal weapons, chalices, and jewelry. Even Pastor Williams was in attendance, dressed as a wandering friar, and he seemed to be thoroughly enjoying himself.

As soon as the feast was announced, everyone found seats at the long tables. As a serving wench—for the evening only, medieval sexist attitudes were allowed!—Robyn joined the others to help bring the food out from the kitchen to the feasters. She was surprisingly happy that Jeff seemed disappointed that she couldn't stay with him. He was left to fend for himself with her mother and father. He seemed a little uneasy, and was being subjected to a determined barrage of talk from her mother.

However, the evening went very well, and Robyn found that all thoughts of death and danger were completely absent from her mind. She helped with the food, exchanging funny double entendres with the "customers," and kept glancing over at Jeff. He was constantly looking in her direction, a sweet, helpless expression on his face, apparently missing her a lot. She smiled and waved at him when she could.

After the food was finished Robyn helped clear the tables; then she was free to join Jeff and her parents. She noted the smug expression on her mother's face and wondered what it meant. What had she missed while she was working? She caught Jeff's eye, and he blushed furiously and glanced away. What did that mean?

The entertainment began. There was a minstrel who sang, accompanying himself on the lute. Then an outrageous juggler/magician, who kept "finding" gold coins tucked down the fronts of women's blouses. A small group of singers followed, then a jester. Finally the two girls dressed as gypsies performed their ever-popular belly dance routine.

That was the only act that Jeff seemed to sit through without looking frequently in Robyn's direction. She had to admit that they were good, but not *that* good.

Thinking about it, she had to confess that he was a nice guy. He was in her thoughts more and more. She was almost certain that he had nothing to do with the murders.

It was that *almost* that bothered her.

What if he really was the killer? Was everything that he said to her nothing but a lie, designed to trap her? She hated all of the indecision. She knew that nothing could spoil a friendship like mistrust. It would be worth almost anything to just be certain.

If Jeff noticed her preoccupation, he didn't say anything. He was too busy watching the belly dancing. Finally, though, it was over, and her parents decided that it was time to leave. As they threaded their way to the door, one of the "gypsy" dancers approached them. In her hand, she held a pack of tarot cards, which she offered to them. Her dark eyes fastened on Jeff.

"Tell your fortune, handsome one?" she murmured mischievously.

Jeff looked startled. "I don't believe in that stuff."

"Nobody does," the girl replied, with a curl to her mouth. "Until they try it. Take a card. What will it be? The King of Cups? The Ace of Wands?" She gave Robyn a sideways glance. "The Lovers?"

"Try it," Robyn urged. "It might be fun."

Jeff shrugged. He reached out and took a card, then turned it over.

It was a black-cloaked skeleton, carrying a scythe. There was just one word on the card: DEATH.

TWENTY

AQUARIUS: *Don't get distracted by others today.*
Trouble comes calling, but avoid it and mind your own
business.

It hadn't been a good weekend for Debi. Preoccupied
with images of the Teen Terror, she had hardly slept at
all. When she had, there were nightmares of finding
Robyn's mutilated body, torn apart by a lion. And when
she had talked with Robyn on Sunday morning, Robyn
had reluctantly told her about the tarot-card incident.
She said it was meaningless, but Debi could hear the
uncertainty even over the phone.

Something had to be done.

Debi had tried talking to her parents, but they
thought her theories about the murders were just wild
speculation. Like everyone else in town, they were certain that the reign of terror was over with Derek behind
bars.

Then Debi had called Dana and received more bad news. Her friend had been out skating the previous evening and had slipped, badly spraining her ankle. She was going to be out of school for the rest of the week.

Now it was Monday morning. And if she and Robyn were right, one more day to the next death. It was not a good way to start the week. Neither of them could concentrate in class and they were glad when it was lunch. They went outside, lost in their glum mood.

"I feel so helpless," Debi said. "Nobody will listen to us."

"Jeff called me yesterday," Robyn told her. "There are just four Leo girls in our year. I called the other three up and told them to stay home tomorrow night. I think I scared them enough so that they won't go out. Maybe that will be enough."

"Maybe not. Natalie was murdered in her own room, with her parents downstairs."

"Well, what can we do?" Robyn demanded. "It's the uncertainty that's killing me. What if we're wrong, and Derek *is* the killer?"

"We're *not* wrong about that," Debi said. "Your horoscope column was changed after he was in jail. No, the killer's still loose. And—I still figure Jeff's the prime suspect."

"And I'm still sure he's innocent," Robyn insisted—though, in her heart, she knew this wasn't exactly true. She *wanted* him to be innocent, but was that enough?

"All right," Debi said, in a sudden burst of fire. "Let's prove it."

"How?"

"Well, the murders all took place after eight at night.

Why don't we watch Jeff's house together tomorrow night? If he's the killer, he'll have to go out, and then we can follow him and call the police."

Robyn said uncertainly, "But that could be dangerous. Especially since I'm on the list of possible victims."

"It's the only way we can ever be certain about him," Debi pointed out. "If we stay home, there *could* be another murder, and then we still won't be sure. And I'll be with you all evening. We should be safe enough like that."

"I don't know," Robyn said. "It seems so risky . . ."

"Would you rather leave your boyfriend on the suspect list?"

"He's not my boyfriend," Robyn protested. Then she shook her head. "No. No, I wouldn't." She looked at Debi and smiled grimly. "Okay. Let's do it. This way, we can prove that Jeff is innocent." She thought for a moment. "How about I ask my parents if I can sleep over at your place tomorrow night? That way, we can get out together easier, since Jeff's just a couple of blocks from you."

"Great. I'll clear it with my folks." Debi grinned. "We'll just go out for tacos or something at eight, and take our time . . ."

Their mood lightened considerably with the knowledge that they would not simply be sitting around all Tuesday night, waiting—either for the killer to come calling, or for news of another victim. Debi could only pray that they had made the right decision, and that she hadn't talked Robyn into a position of greater danger.

* * *

Tuesday was one of the longest days of Debi's life. Classes dragged on and on, and she couldn't hide her interest in the clock. Finally school was over and they headed for their lockers. Jeff was waiting there for them, and Debi's heart almost skipped a beat. If Robyn was as nervous, she hid it well.

"Hi, guys," Jeff greeted them. "Uh, Robyn, I've got a lot of work to do tonight. I'm a bit behind. I know I was supposed to call you and talk about the computer program, but I don't know if I'll have time for it today."

On a sudden inspiration, Debi said, "She's sleeping over at my house tonight anyway. We'll probably be up all night with girl talk. You know how it is."

He grinned shyly. "Not really. What do you talk about?"

"Anything and everything," replied Robyn. "All sorts of things that we don't want other people to hear."

"Probably dissecting me behind my back," he said, laughing. He sounded nervous, though. Was it just because of his natural shyness, or some other reason? With a wave, he quickly walked off.

Debi watched him go. "Pretty suspicious, if you ask me."

"What?" Robyn looked amazed. "What are you talking about?"

"That he asked you not to call him tonight of all nights, for one thing. And for another—how come he didn't offer to walk us to my house? It's on his way home, after all. And if he likes you as we think he does, wouldn't he look for any excuse to hang around with you?"

Robyn looked uncertain. "Maybe he's just preoccupied. He could be telling the truth."

"And he could be lying through his teeth," Debi added. "But tonight we'll know for sure."

As they were leaving the school, they saw Joe Butler starting to empty the trash from the wastebaskets. He waved at them. "I'm dropping by to see your father later," he told Robyn. "He's promised to do a special candle sculpture and I want to talk about it with him. Would you mind telling him?"

"Well, I would," she replied, "but I'm staying with Debi tonight. I could call him, though."

"No, that's okay." Joe grinned. "I'll give him a buzz later, when I'm done here."

A sudden thought struck Robyn. "Are you who he's doing the Vlad piece for?"

Joe nodded. "I've been fascinated with vampires since I was a kid. Bela Lugosi and all that. I guess I just never grew up. I wanted something special to add to my collection—something that nobody else has. Something unique, you know?"

As they left the building, Robyn sighed. "Poor old Joe is out of luck again."

"What do you mean?"

"Dad's decided that he can't do the piece." Robyn shrugged. "Dad's really anti-violence, you know, and he just can't work up any enthusiasm for the job. You know, I'm a little worried about him."

Debi liked Robyn's father—he was cheerful, witty, and concerned about his daughter—almost the exact opposite of her own father. "Why? What's wrong?"

"He's been overworking lately. Sometimes when I get

153

home, he's upstairs, sleeping in the day, which isn't like him. And he's been kind of moody, too. He's been getting horrible migraine headaches—tension, sort of." She sighed. "I think he needs a vacation. We all do. Mom hasn't taken any time off from the store in almost a year."

"Well, maybe you can work on them," suggested Debi. "Play on their sympathies and beg to get away from it all."

"Yeah. Maybe." Robyn didn't sound too certain.

Debi's parents seemed to be oblivious to the girls' nervousness that night. Debi was certain that a blind man a mile away could see that they were up to something, but neither her mother nor father seemed to think that they had anything on their minds. After a quiet meal which the girls hardly ate, Debi led the way upstairs.

Robyn had dropped her overnight bag off when they had picked up Debi that morning. Mrs. Smolinske had moved a camp bed into Debi's room, which was large enough to house a small army, anyway. To try to pass the time, Robyn laid her nightclothes out on the bed, and then kept rearranging them nervously.

In the silence that neither of them wanted to break, Debi simply sat on her bed and worried. Normally, the two of them had riotous evenings together, but this night would not be one of them.

Eventually, the clock told them it was seven-thirty. They looked at one another.

"Time to start out, I guess," Robyn said. She looked

pale and distracted. "Uh—after one more pit stop, that is." She dived into the bathroom.

Debi stood up, shaking slightly. Were they being incredibly stupid to do this? She took a flashlight from her closet and stuck it into her largest handbag, which she slung over her shoulder. It didn't look too suspicious—she hoped. Then she paced the room until Robyn reappeared.

"Sorry," her friend apologized. "It's just nerves." She looked as if she was on the verge of calling the whole thing off. Debi wasn't certain herself that she would be able to go through with it. Then Robyn steeled herself. "Let's go."

They went downstairs and Debi poked her head into the living room. "Uh—Robyn and I are just going to get ourselves some tacos," she announced, breaking out into a sweat. "We may be a while."

"I'm not surprised," her mother replied. "The two of you hardly ate any dinner. All right, be careful."

"Don't worry," Debi promised. "We will be."

It was a short walk to the block where the Goldstein house stood. They kept well back, but where they could have a clear view of the house. They were out of the direct line Jeff would have to take to go to Debi's house. There were two lights on that they could see.

"Now we wait," Debi said, glancing at her watch.

"And pray nothing happens," agreed Robyn.

It was very hard on their nerves, and neither of them could think of anything to talk about. They both kept casting their eyes at their watches.

At just after eight, they tensed. One of the lights in

155

the Goldstein house went out. A moment later the front door opened and Jeff came out.

"It doesn't mean anything," Robyn said, in a low whisper, even though there was no way he could hear them.

Just as quietly, Debi said, "Well, we'll follow him and see where's he's going. I deliberately told him you were staying with me—so if he heads toward my house, we'll know he's up to no good."

Robyn nodded, and they watched Jeff walk quickly down the street. They slipped in behind him, keeping back and close to the shadows, but Jeff never looked back.

Debi nudged Robyn in the ribs, more certain than ever.

He was heading straight for the Smolinske house.

TWENTY-ONE

LEO: *Your worst nightmares come true. Positive thinking won't help here.*

Robyn held her breath, her heart beating furiously. *She'd been wrong after all! Jeff was the one who—*

Jeff reached the Smolinske house, stopped, looked at it, and then walked right past it.

Robyn let her breath out in a rush, feeling almost dizzy with relief. "He didn't stop!"

"So where's he going?" asked Debi, sounding a little unsure. "It can't just be a coincidence he's out tonight."

"Come on," Robyn said, and they set off after Jeff again. They were both wearing sneakers and dark-colored clothing. Keeping to the shadows and lurking for heart-wrenching seconds behind trees, they kept on his trail. He never looked back, but if he did, he probably wouldn't have seen them anyway.

157

It wasn't long before they realized that there was just one place he could be heading.

"School," Debi said quietly. "That's strange." After a moment's thought, she added, "Then again, he may be using it as a sort of base. He couldn't hide any murder weapons at home, could he?"

"Oh, be quiet," Robyn said, but she had to admit that Jeff was acting pretty weird.

At the main doors, Jeff looked around for the first time. Robyn and Debi ducked into the shadows of the school wall, and to their relief he didn't seem to have spotted them. Then Jeff bent over the lock and did something.

The door swung open and he slipped inside.

"Now what?" asked Robyn.

"Let's take a look," Debi suggested. "At the very least, he's guilty of breaking and entering."

They walked quickly to the door. Robyn glanced around, feeling half foolish, half guilty herself. Was this really a wise move? Thankfully, there was no one in sight. Had there been, she was sure she'd have freaked out.

"Unlocked," Debi said with satisfaction. "He's left himself a way out. And us a way in."

"Oh, no," Robyn said quickly. "I think this has gone far enough. Let's call the police right now."

"The closest phone is by the lockers," Debi pointed out. "We can use that one if he hasn't gone near them. It's much faster. Otherwise he might even be gone by the time the police arrive."

"All right," Robyn said dubiously. She felt bad about

158

calling the police on Jeff in the first place, and had to admit that she'd prefer to delay the call if she could.

Inside, school seemed very different from the cheery place of the day. Shadows stretched across the corridors and the classrooms yawned like caves. Debi tapped her arm and pointed. Ahead of them there was a faint light.

"Let's take a look," she whispered. "Maybe we'll get an idea of what's going on."

As they drew closer, the two girls saw that the light was coming from the steps down to the basement. Robyn drew the line here and grabbed Debi.

"That's enough," she said quietly. "Go back to the phone and call the sheriff. I'll stay here, and if I hear him coming up the steps, I'll shut him in. That way, we'll be certain he's trapped for when they come."

Debi nodded and scuttled off down the dark corridor.

Left alone, Robyn began to have grave doubts. It was scary to be here in the school with Jeff so close. She still had trouble believing he was the killer—but what other explanation for his actions was there? If only she could be *certain* . . . She couldn't stand not knowing. It was agony. She really wanted to trust Jeff, to get to know him better. But not if he was a killer.

There was a sharp noise from below, and Jeff's muffled curse.

Unable to help herself any longer, Robyn opened the door slightly and peered into the lighted stairwell. There was a sharp turn at the bottom of the stairs that led to the storage areas and Joe's little rooms, so she was unable to see any more. But she had to know . . . had she trusted a murderer for the past several weeks? What was making him do this?

159

Slowly, her heart in her mouth, Robyn began to gingerly descend. An inner voice screamed at her that she was being stupid, but she didn't care. She just wanted to be certain. She had to see what Jeff was doing. After all, maybe he'd hurt himself down there. If he was innocent and injured, would she ever forgive herself for not helping him out? She had to believe he was innocent. She had to.

Finally, after nervous long minutes, Robyn reached the foot of the stairs. Carefully, she peered around the frame of the door.

Jeff was in Joe's room, looking through the various boxes there. They were stacked along and under the metal shelving that lined two of the walls. None of the boxes was labeled, and he was obviously looking for something.

Jeff was only about ten feet from her, but completely preoccupied with his search. Robyn couldn't understand what he was doing. Biting her lower lip, she inched forward for a better look.

Then her foot snagged on something that rattled away from her. With a startled cry, she grabbed the closest wall for support. Jeff froze and whipped around, staring at her with an expression she'd never seen before. Gathering the last of her wits, she turned to run, but Jeff was far too fast. As she started up the stairs, she felt his hand around her ankle. He pulled. With a wild cry, she fell backward. Jeff's hand snaked around her neck and dragged her head back.

For one terrible second, she stared into his face, and realized that she was dead. Everything she hadn't wanted to believe about him was true.

Then Jeff let up on his grip, shock written all over his face. "Robyn!" he exclaimed. "What the hell do you think you're doing?"

Robyn pulled herself free and backed against the wall, looking around wildly for anything she could use as a weapon. "Don't touch me!" she warned him. "Debi's already called the cops!"

"What on earth are you talking . . . ?" he began, then went ashen. "You don't think—you couldn't think that I'm the killer! Robyn, how could you?" He looked shocked and hurt.

Hardly daring to believe it, she said, slowly, "You're not?"

"How could you even think that? I thought—I thought we were friends. I thought maybe . . ."

"We *are* friends. I like you a lot," she told him, hardly daring to believe what he was telling her. "But . . . well, I wasn't certain that you were innocent. Debi was sure you were the killer, and I wanted to be as sure you weren't. Then, tonight of all nights, you pulled this . . . this whatever it is you're up to."

Jeff started to look more hopeful. "You didn't really think it was me?"

Robyn shook her head. "I was just afraid I was wrong. I'm sorry, Jeff."

Jeff came toward her slowly, a shy smile on his face. Robyn waited, her heart in her throat, as he bent his head down to hers. He kissed her softly. Robyn responded from pure relief and the happiness that he wasn't the killer. She'd been right to trust him. Everything would be fine. . . .

After a long moment, he let her go. He gazed down

into her face and she could read the joy and wonder in his eyes. Robyn felt a thousand different emotions all at once: surprise, happiness, relief . . .

"What did you mean about *tonight of all nights?*" he asked her.

"Tonight's when the next killing is supposed to be," she told him. Then she realized that she had never explained about the link with her column, thanks to Debi's suspicions. She explained now.

"Damn!" Jeff said furiously. "That had never occurred to me. But—you're a Leo. That means you're in danger! I've got to get you out of here."

"What do you mean? If it isn't you, it must be Derek."

Jeff shook his head, then seemed to come to a decision. "Did you say the police were on their way? Quick —help me search Joe's room. If what I'm looking for is there, we may be able to explain things to the sheriff."

Robyn followed him into the room and started to open the boxes on the shelves. "What are we looking for?"

"The written school files," Jeff told her. "I realized that our one-track concentration on the fact that the files are computerized now made us forget that they were also written at one time."

"Well, Debi and I already guessed that," Robyn told him. "I asked Joe about it. But he burned them years ago when they went onto computer."

"Robyn," Jeff said patiently, "I'm crazy about you, but for a smart girl, you can be pretty dumb some days. Joe *said* he'd burned them. What if he hasn't?"

He is crazy about me, Robyn thought happily. Then the chill from what else he had said settled in. "If the

162

files are still intact," she whispered, "it means that Joe is the killer." Then, thinking about it, she remembered that Joe had also burned the altered prediction . . . and hung around the lockers . . . and read her astrology column.

It was true . . .

"Right," Jeff agreed. "So keep on looking."

She did. After a second, she asked, "But why do *you* think it might be Joe?"

"Those photos in Derek's locker," he explained. "Joe has the master keys to all of the lockers—remember? He could have hidden them there. And Derek used to take the history elective until last year, but he dropped it this year. If Joe's working from the old records, he wouldn't have known that."

"Oh." Robyn felt really stupid for not having figured that out. "So why didn't you tell me this before? And what was that excuse about work tonight?"

"Because you're a Leo, and the next victim will be a Leo. I wanted to keep you out of trouble, especially after that tarot-card reading on Saturday. I was terrified that it meant I was going to get you killed. And if I'd known about your column being the key, I'd have been even more scared."

She smiled and touched his arm affectionately. "Poor Jeff." How could she have ever thought he was a computer nerd?

"Poor you. Keep looking."

They finished the boxes but there was no sign of any files. Uncertainly, Robyn glanced at Jeff. He stood undecided for a moment, then grabbed the old, rolled-up carpet from the corner. "Worth a shot," he said, and grabbed the edge. With a flick of his wrists, he let it unroll.

Robyn gasped.

On the carpet was painted a large circle in gold. It was cut into twelve segments, and onto each segment had been painted a sign of the Zodiac. Under these, attached to the material, were old manila envelopes. The first four signs had no envelopes.

She and Jeff bent to look closer. Under a crude painting of a ram was pinned a photograph of Jenny Warren's dead body. Then, next to it, Alan's blood-soaked form. Then Natalie's garroted corpse, propped against her mirror. Finally, Ryan's shattered body.

Robyn felt like throwing up. They were the worst pictures she'd ever seen in her life. She clutched at the wall for support. Grimly, Jeff pulled the envelope from under the stylized lion and tore it open.

Robyn's own file lay exposed.

Stunned by the shock of it, Robyn didn't hear the noise until too late. By the time she turned, the intruder had smashed his fist down on Jeff's exposed neck, dropping him senseless to the carpet.

Joe Butler smiled down at her, but there was no warmth in the smile at all.

TWENTY-TWO

Terrified, Robyn backed away from him. But there was only a short space before she ran into the wall of shelves and had to stop. She tried to swallow, torn between facing Joe and trying to see if Jeff was still alive.

Joe moved slightly, bringing up the hand he'd used to hit Jeff. He unclenched his fist and Robyn saw that he was wearing a huge, furry glove. Set into the fingertips were clawlike blades.

"Leo," he said. "The lion." He flexed his hand and the blades glittered in the faint light from the doorway. "The right way for you to die." He stepped over Jeff, his eyes blazing.

"Joe," Robyn managed to croak, unable to think of anything to save herself. "Don't do it. Think!"

"I *have* thought!" he told her. "I've done almost nothing but think! Now, I have to act."

"Joe, I thought we were friends!"

He looked hurt. "We *are* friends," he replied. "There's

nothing personal about this. But I have to do it." His face seemed twisted in on itself, as if he was arguing with something inside of his mind. Maybe he really didn't want to hurt her, but something was forcing him on.

Hope began to flicker in Robyn's mind. Maybe, just maybe, he could still be reached and she could keep him talking until the police arrived. He seemed hurt by her accusation, so she prodded him further. "But if you don't want to kill me, Joe, why do you think you have to?"

"Because you'll be helping me," he said, his eyes flickering around as if there were several people there, watching him. *Haunted by his other victims?* "You want to help me, don't you? You're my friend."

"Yes, Joe," Robyn said gently, fighting down her panic and disgust. "I'm your friend. I want to help. But if you explain to me, I'll be able to help you much better, won't I?" *Come on, damn you—talk!*

Joe hesitated and looked at his glove. Then he sighed. "All right," he agreed. "Maybe you will understand. I don't want to hurt you. If I explain, then will you let me kill you? I'll be quick," he promised. "I don't want you to suffer." He seemed almost pathetically wanting her to approve.

"That's kind of you, Joe." The sarcasm seemed to be lost on him. "I'll listen, I promise."

He nodded, and to her relief he stood still. She couldn't tear her eyes away from the glove. He kept flexing his fingers nervously as he talked. He was still just inside the doorway, and he paced up and down the three steps in each direction he could walk. Robyn forced herself to focus all of her attention on him, as much as she wanted to look at Jeff.

166

He was on his face on the floor, not moving. Joe never spared him a second glance. *Was he dead, or badly injured, or what?*

"I've never had any luck, you know," Joe said earnestly. "Never. When I was a kid, my parents were too poor to send me to college. So I joined the Army. You know, get a scholarship and all that? I thought that way I'd get to study and end up with a great job, and a family, and everything. But I was really dumb, you know. Because Fate wasn't going to let me win like that.

"Then came the Vietnam War, and I thought that was my chance. I could be a hero, get battlefield promotions, maybe a good rank. That would have been perfect. But it didn't happen."

"Why not, Joe?" *Just a little while longer, and the police were bound to come . . .*

"Because I wasn't sent to Vietnam. Oh, no, not me! Everybody else went there, but I went to Germany as part of the peacekeeping force. Miles and miles from any action, stuck in a useless job again. Then, as if that wasn't bad enough, there was a damned terrorist attack. They bombed the barracks, killed a few people. But not me—I wasn't even lucky enough to die. I just got hurt." He tapped his leg. "There's still a load of shrapnel in here. It hurts like crazy in the winter, and I can't stop that pain. I can't move my right knee at all." He was almost in tears, lost in the injustices that had happened to him.

"But even that wasn't the end. I was invalided out of the Army, on account of my leg. But I didn't get the scholarship because I hadn't served long enough!" He spat on the floor, narrowly missing Jeff's still body. "It

167

was all downhill from there. I moved back to town and the only job I could get was as janitor in my old school. Me, cleaning up behind a bunch of spoiled, privileged kids who all had more luck than me. I watched them all graduate and go on to colleges. They got great jobs and earned lots of money. And I just worked myself to death here. It just wasn't fair. None of it was fair!"

He looked at her and there was a dangerous glint in his eyes. "But then everything changed. Suddenly, I realized that I had a mission in life. The gods of the Zodiac had knocked me down, cursed all of my luck, and brought me here. But not because I was despised and rejected. No. It was because they needed an agent. Someone who would listen to them and do their bidding. For so long, they had been neglected. They needed a devotee. It was then that I heard the voice of the prophetess, and I realized that I had been called to serve the gods of the Zodiac."

"Prophetess?" Robyn was following most of his story, but this was a new twist.

"Yes." He smiled happily. "The school newspaper started to run a column she wrote—Jean Stephenson. And there, on the very first day, my fortune read: *Seize the day! Make those necessary changes in your life!* I knew it was a message from the gods to me."

Stunned, Robyn could only stare at him. *He doesn't even know it's me!* she realized. *He thinks she's a messenger from the Zodiac!* She couldn't even remember making that prediction. It was so generalized, but he had seen some strange light of revelation in it.

"That was when I knew what my purpose was," he told her. "I had kept all the files of the students when I was ordered to destroy them. I didn't know why at first —I would just read through them, and hate those kids for being who they were. Then the answer came to me.

"All I had to do was to transfer their good luck to me! If I killed one person from each sign of the Zodiac, using the weapons that the gods would reveal to me, when the wheel of fortune was completed, I would have all of the luck that they had forfeited through death! And the gods would have the sacrifices they wanted.

"It was so simple. I was amazed I had never seen it before. So I prepared and planned, and when the first one, Aries, was ready, I waited for the sign from the prophetess. It came, and I took Jenny Warren as the first victim."

He sighed, clearly thinking back on that night. "I was very careful," he explained. "I didn't hurt her too much. After all, she was doing me a favor, and the gods only ask for sacrifice, not pain. So you won't need to worry when your time comes." He smiled gently. "I'll be very careful, I promise. You'll hardly feel anything when you die."

Robyn was still sick with fear. He hadn't forgotten his purpose in being here. But what was keeping the police? Why hadn't they arrived yet? She wished she dared look at her watch, to see how long it had been. Maybe she just thought it had been ages, and it really hadn't. But she couldn't take her eyes away from Joe.

"Now,' he told her, raising his hand. "Why don't you just lie down on the carpet, nice and easy? And close your eyes." He smiled. "This will probably be the best of all of the sacrifices. Your blood can mingle with the Zodiac, instead of it having to be just a picture."

TWENTY-THREE

As she faced her death only seconds away, sudden clarity seemed to penetrate Robyn's mind. "But what about Jeff?" she asked gently. "He's an Aquarius. If you kill him, it'll all go wrong on you. You have to do it right, don't you? Otherwise it won't work." *Humor him, play on his insane fantasy . . .*

"Yeah, that's right," he agreed thoughtfully. "If I killed him, then I'd have to start all over again."

He said "if," Robyn thought wildly. *Then Jeff's still alive!*

"On the other hand," Joe said thoughtfully, "there's Debi Smolinske, too. I can't leave her now, either." He saw the shock in Robyn's eyes and laughed. "Oh! I get it! You were trying to keep me talking till the police arrived!" Shaking his head, he smiled. "She never did get to call them. I followed you both here from her house. It was easy—you never really looked back. Then, when you split up, I knew where she was going. So I locked her away first, then came to deal with you. Well, let's get your part over with. Then I'll worry about the other two." He flexed his fingers and there was a smile of anticipation on his face.

Nothing had changed in his mind, Robyn realized. And the sheriff hadn't been warned at all. Terror was eating at her. She knew she was just seconds away from being murdered. She felt stunned, defeated, without a hope. Like Joe had felt before he had read her column. If only Jeff was awake, maybe together they could—

Her column!

"Joe, you've made a very big mistake," she said gently.

He thought for a moment. "No, not a one. I've been very careful."

"You've made one big mistake," she insisted. "You can't kill me: I'm the prophetess."

He stopped, stock-still, and glared at her. "No, you aren't! Jean Stephenson is!"

"*I'm* Jean Stephenson," she told him. "It's just a pen name I use."

"No!" he cried, confusion on his face. "No! You're lying! You're not going to try and cheat me now. I gotta kill you!"

"If you kill me, Joe," she said quietly, gently, "then who will tell you when to kill the other victims? And if you kill *me*—the one who speaks for the gods of the Zodiac—then the gods will be very unhappy with you."

He went ashen at the thought. "No," he repeated, "you're lying. You gotta be. You're not the prophetess." But it sounded as if he was fighting against some inner certainty that she was telling the truth. He seemed to be

171

hearing voices that she could not. Robyn vaguely remembered reading once that many schizophrenics heard voices telling them what to do. Was this what was happening to Joe?

"Yes, I am, Joe." Convinced she'd hit his weak spot, she kept hammering on. "And I can prove it. You changed my prophecy for today, didn't you?"

"It was your fault," he said. "You were trying to cheat me. I always looked for the prophecies as soon as you wrote them out." With a chill of hope, Robyn realized that he seemed to have accepted that she was Jean Stephenson. "I found the paper when I looked at the manuscript last week. I saw what you did, so I changed it back."

"You cheated the Zodiac, Joe," she told him. Would he believe this part? "The gods of the Zodiac told me to change it, that I'd made a mistake. I changed it for them, and you changed it back. They didn't want you to kill me, Joe. Surely you can see that? They were trying to save you from this terrible mistake. You tried to cheat them, and they don't like that."

"No," he said, almost in a whisper. "No . . . they speak to me. They never told me that they spoke to *you*. Except when you wrote down their prophecies."

"How could I write their words if I didn't hear them speak?" Robyn was clutching at anything she could to stop him. Maybe it would be too much for him and his mind would give out. Maybe he'd just let her go. Maybe she'd think of some way to beat him.

Joe looked at her, shaking his head. The fanatical light in his eyes still burned. His fingers in that terrible glove jerked spasmodically. He didn't seem to be able to control himself.

Struck by sudden inspiration, Robyn asked softly, "What's your sign, Joe? Who's your own god?"

White-faced, he staggered back against the doorway. "Leo . . ." he mumbled. "But they can't want *me* as a sacrifice. They can't. I've been good. I've done what they wanted."

"You failed them, Joe," she insisted. "You wanted to kill me, and you wouldn't accept their correction. Now you have to pay for it."

"No!" he cried, feeding on the inner fears and voices. "It must be you." He glared at her crazily. "It has to be you. *You* tried to cheat them, to change their plans." He seemed to fold in on himself somehow, listening to those insane voices in his head that nobody else could ever hear. A grin stole across his features and he began to lick his lips.

"You betrayed them!" he told her. "You changed their words, and you have now been rejected by them. You must die."

"Then who will speak for them, Joe?" she asked frantically. "Who will show you the way?"

He shrugged. "They can pick someone else. They can do anything they want. But now they want you—as a sacrifice. But not easily, no. Not now. You've got to pay for betraying them and me. You've got to suffer!"

With a snarl, he jumped at her. Robyn screamed and tried to dodge the blow he aimed for her with his artificial paw. She almost made it. As she dived under his arms, he struck out, and she felt the blades slashing through her top and in lines of fire down her back.

Then she was past him and free. Her back burned and she felt the blood trickling down her skin, soaking her top. Pain lanced through her muscles.

Joe cursed and spun around. Robyn could see the bright redness of her blood dripping from the claw. Almost unthinkingly, she grabbed some of the cleaning bottles from his shelves and started to throw them at him. He slashed out, ripping through the plastic of the bottle she had thrown. Instantly, the air was filled with the acrid, burning stench of ammonia.

Coughing and hacking, her eyes stinging, she backed out of Joe's room. She could hear him heaving, too.

She had to get out of the basement! Hardly able to see, she staggered to the stairs and started to climb them. Her eyes were streaming, her back a mass of pain. But she knew that if she stopped now, she was dead.

Scrambling to the top of the stairs, she tried to open the door.

It was locked.

Hearing movement at the bottom of the stairs, she twisted around. She whimpered from the agony in her back. Wiping at his eyes, Joe snarled, "There's no escape for you. I locked the door on my way down. Only by your death will you get out of here."

Terrified, Robyn watched as he started to climb the stairs toward her. He had the claw raised, her blood already drying on it.

"You're gonna pay for what you've done," he promised her. "You're gonna pay for every last bit. You heard the voices, too, and you rejected them. Now you're gonna taste their revenge."

174

TWENTY-FOUR

There was nowhere left to run now. Robyn pressed back against the door, but her wounds forced her forward again. She couldn't stand the pain—and what difference did it make, anyway? There was no escape.

"Leave her alone, Butler."

Jeff! She looked past Joe, now halfway up to her. Jeff was standing, reeling, at the bottom of the stairs. In his hand he held a large hammer from Joe's tool kit. Dizzily, she realized that the ammonia breaking in the room below must have woken him up! And not a second too soon.

Snarling, Joe took in the new threat. He'd lucked out before by getting Jeff when he wasn't looking. But now it would be much more even . . .

He made his mind up in a second. Howling, Joe jumped up the stairs and struck out at Robyn. Not to kill, to hurt. She flung up her left arm and the vicious claw raked across it, ripping at her flesh. With a scream of pain she lost her balance, and Joe pushed her down. She hardly felt the blow as she hit the bottom stairs, and then Jeff grabbed hold of her.

"You haven't won!" Joe screamed. "I've still got that Smolinske girl! She'll make a perfect sacrifice for the gods. If it's done right, maybe they'll help me out here . . ." He unlocked the door and dived through it.

Robyn managed to sit up and heard the key turn in the lock behind him. Her back was one blistering mass of pain, and now her left arm was leaving a trail of blood and throbbing in agony. Jeff didn't look much better than her. He had several gashes across his neck. His clothes reeked of ammonia.

"You okay?" he gasped, trying to figure out where he could touch her and not hurt her. She shook her head.

"No. But Debi's in a worse spot right now." Robyn spoke quickly, looking at the locked door. "Joe's gone completely over the edge now. He's hearing voices that tell him to kill people. He thinks they demand sacrifices. Now that he's lost me, he's probably going after her, hoping that even though she's not a Leo, these sadistic gods of his might accept her blood for the moment. We have to help her."

Jeff pushed past her and ran to the top step. Taking a breath, he swung the hammer hard against the lock. There was a cracking sound, but little else. "That hurt," he said, gritting his teeth. Then he tried again.

It took four more blows, and Robyn could see the rawness and blood on his hands after the final blow sent the door crashing open. "Where is she?" he asked her.

"Debi went to the phones," Robyn said as they

staggered out of the stairway and into the darkened corridors. "Where could he have locked her up?"

"The boys' room," Jeff said, after thinking a moment. "He's going to sacrifice her. What's her sign?"

"Aquarius."

"Terrific. He'll probably try and drown her in the toilet." Jeff set off as fast as he could. Despite the pain in her back and arm, Robyn managed to stay with him.

When they reached the boys' room, Jeff kicked hard at the door. It slammed open and they both shot in.

Empty.

But on the floor was Debi's bag, its contents spilled out.

"They were here," Robyn cried. "But where could they have gone?"

They heard the front door of the school slam faintly. Jeff looked at her. "Out of school," he said. "Water. Where?"

Robyn tried to think, but it was hard to concentrate. Her ears were buzzing and she was seeing bright yellow jags of light flashing in front of her eyes. How much blood had she lost? Was she going to faint now and not be able to help her friend? Fighting back the nausea and pain, she said, "The little lake—you know, where we caught the frogs for biology!"

"Right!" He kissed her, fast, on the cheek. "Smart girl. Stay here. I'll stop him."

"No," Robyn insisted, running with him to the door. "Debi's my friend. I can't let her down."

He didn't bother to argue.

TWENTY-FIVE

AQUARIUS: A time to stick with friends. Avoid exercise, and feeling sorry for yourself.

Debi had sat in the boys' rest room for what had seemed like hours. She had been grabbed from behind on her way to the phones and thrown inside. She'd just caught a glimpse of Joe Butler as he had slammed the door on her, then locked it.

She knew he was going after Robyn now. They had stupidly walked right into this!

Was her best friend dead, while she was stuck in here? It was obvious that as soon as Robyn was dead, Debi was bound to be the next victim. She was one of those people who proverbially knew too much.

There was no way out of the small room. Two stalls, a couple of troughs, and the sinks. There was only one window, much too small for her to get through. Maybe she could break it and scream for help. But it faced across the school playing fields. No one could hear her over that distance. There was nothing she could do.

She looked around the room. There were scrawled comments all over the place. Most were crude, graphic, and probably impossible to perform. Over one of the toilet roll holders, someone had written: "Sociology degrees. Please take one."

Terrific. Nothing of any use to her at all. If only she or Robyn had brought some kind of weapon or—

The flashlight!

Scattering the contents of her bag on the floor, she pulled the light out and tested it. It shone brightly enough, maybe. The little window in the wall was high, but if she stood on the urinal . . . Wrinkling her nose in distaste, she tried it. It wasn't easy. The whole thing wobbled as she pulled herself up, but she made it. Reaching upward, she could hold the flashlight level with the glass. Hanging on to the water pipe with her left hand, she smashed the butt of the torch against the glass. There was a breaking sound, and a couple of shards fell into her hair. Most fell outside, though. Looking up, she reversed the flashlight and started to turn it on and off.

Morse code—three long, three short, three long. Thank God for the Girl Scouts! Now, if only somebody happened to see the signal—and also know the SOS sign . . .

She kept signaling until her hand was too cramped to flick the switch any longer. Then, carefully, she switched hands and started up again.

The door suddenly flew open and Joe Butler stormed in.

179

Debi screamed as he came for her. He wore some funny kind of glove with knives—like he'd been playing *Nightmare On Elm Street* or something—and blood was dripping from it.

He'd killed Robyn! And she was next!

With a scream, she jumped right at him, trying to use the flashlight as a club. She hit his arm and he yelled, but he grabbed her with his free hand, his fingers winding in her hair. He jerked her head back, and she was certain he was going to rip her throat out with the glove.

Instead, he tossed the glove aside and dragged her painfully to him. "Why are you being so difficult?" he snarled. "Accept your fate." Then he chopped his hand down, hard, on the side of her neck. He'd been trained in the military and had learned some lessons well.

Debi lost consciousness completely.

The old pond didn't have good memories for Robyn. It was less than half a mile from the school, and was actually almost a small lake. One side of it was a reed bed, which the local frogs adored. As a result, the biology teacher inevitably took the kids down there to collect frogs for dissection.

Robyn had point-blank refused to do it. Debi, Dana, and Natalie had backed her up, and all four had quietly been given a different assignment to do.

Now, in a grisly turn of events, the pond that so many kids had taken frogs from to murder was about to be the scene of the murder of one of the students—unless they could stop it.

It seemed to take forever to reach the pond. Every

inch of the way, Robyn could only pray that she'd guessed correctly where Joe, his mind torn by fear, pain, and impending defeat, had decided to make his sacrifice. If she had guessed wrong, Debi was already dead.

"Ahead," Jeff gasped. He looked drained, too, but just as determined to keep going.

She followed his wavering finger. She had guessed right.

Joe had just reached the pond, Debi slung over one shoulder. *Dead?* No, it couldn't be—she *must* just be unconscious! As they watched, still racing as fast as they could, Joe threw Debi to the ground, then dragged her head under the murky water.

Jeff seemed to draw on some inner energy and he managed to wring a little more speed from his legs. Determined to do her share, Robyn battled down the pain, the weariness, and the burning ache in her chest, and stretched out as hard as she could to keep pace with him. Neither of them slowed down as they reached the pond.

With more of an uncontrolled fall than a tackle, Jeff threw himself at Joe. He hit the unwary custodian hard in the back. With a cry of shock, rage, and fear, Joe was knocked into the pond, Jeff tumbling after him. Robyn collapsed by the edge of the pond, hysterically grabbing Debi's limp form and dragging her out of the filthy water. Water streamed off her friend's face and a trickle ran from the edge of her mouth.

God! Let her be alive! Robyn prayed, and felt for Debi's heartbeat. It was there, but very weak. Should she try mouth-to-mouth? Or was that only when the heart stopped? Robyn couldn't recall. Debi had been the Girl Scout, not her!

With a spasm, Debi coughed, spitting out water, and then started to choke. Ignoring her own pain, Robyn managed to get Debi into a sitting position and started thumping her on the back. Gasping and coughing, Debi seemed to be coming around.

As soon as she was sure Debi could stay upright on her own, Robyn let go of her. Kicking off her shoes and ignoring Debi's choked protests, Robyn waded out to see if she could help Jeff. His lack of experience at fighting was telling on him. Fueled by terror, panic, and anger, Joe was striking wildly out, but he had been trained.

Joe managed to get in one blow to Jeff's stomach that left him reeling and gasping. The custodian turned to try to make a run for it, then saw Robyn. He was panting, bent over from the strain, and drawn by the fear that was eating at his insides. "I can't hear them," he whispered desperately. "I can't hear them . . ." Then, as a flicker of some kind of sanity passed through him once more, he seemed to focus on her. "Let me by," he gasped, "and I won't hurt you."

Robyn looked at him—the man who had killed her friends, who had tried to murder Debi, and who had almost killed her. The man who had framed Derek and tried to smash Jeff into a pulp. Something inside of her snapped. All of her belief in non-violence was forgotten in a second. "You bastard," she hissed, and swung hard with everything in her. "You'll never hurt anyone again!"

The blow caught him on the side of the head. It wasn't well aimed, but it had all her hatred, all her fear, and all of her remaining strength in it. That was more than enough.

With a cry, Joe toppled backward and vanished under the water. He'd stumbled so far out, he must have gone into a hole. He'd be no danger for a minute, at least.

The fury inside Robyn seemed to die when Joe vanished. She was dimly aware of the pain in her hand from the force of the blow. But compared to everything else she'd suffered, it seemed minor. Heedless of her soaking clothes, she bent to lift Jeff to his feet.

"You okay?" she gasped, shaking the water from her drenched hair.

"Oh, fine," he answered, his voice as weak as hers. But he eyed her with respect. "Remind me never to argue with you," he said. "That was one hell of a right hook."

"I think I broke my hand doing it," she told him, and was only half joking. She looked around, but there was no sign of Joe at all. Could he still be underwater? "I don't see Joe."

"He can't swim," Jeff told her. "That leg of his."

Robyn went white with shock. "Then . . ."

"Yeah. I think he drowned. And good riddance."

Before she could say anything, she heard the scream of sirens and a police car drew up on the edge of the pond. Jeff looked at her and started to laugh.

"Terrific. *Now* the cavalry arrives!"

TWENTY-SIX

LEO & AQUARIUS: Enough hard work—it's time for a rest, and a reevaluation of your life.

It was Sheriff Adkins's generally silent deputy. By the time Robyn and Jeff had made it back to dry land, the officer had already wrapped a blanket around Debi and was calling in for an ambulance and the sheriff. Then he came to help the two of them ashore.

"Don't have any more blankets," he apologized. "You kids okay?"

"We are now," Jeff assured him.

"What in Hades is going on here?" He gestured toward the houses nearby. "We got complaints about vandals at the school playing games, then about a street gang at large. Now I turn up three wet kids."

"It was the Teen Terror," Robyn said helpfully. "It wasn't Derek Vine—it was Joe Butler. He tried to kill me, and Jeff, and Debi."

184

The deputy whistled. "And where is he now?"

Jeff pointed at the pond. "We were fighting, and he never came up."

Eyeing the pond, the officer said, "Have to drag the thing to get his body, I expect. There's sand in the middle there. Caught a few other people like that over the years." He scratched his neck. "You sure about him being the killer?"

"Yes. Definitely," Robyn said. The cold wasn't just in her bones, but in her voice.

"There's proof in his room back at school," added Jeff.

"Well, I guess I'd better call this in," the deputy grunted, heading back for his car.

"It's over," Robyn said, sighing. She tried to examine her feelings, but she was too tired to think straight. She'd killed Joe, hitting him like that, but she couldn't feel it. It had been an accident—she'd never actually wanted to kill him. Maybe later she'd feel some guilt—but right now, she felt only relief.

"Yes," Jeff agreed. "It's over." With his free hand, he turned Robyn's face to his, and kissed her. They were both cold and soaked, but for that moment, Robyn didn't care. Fiercely, she kissed him back, ignoring all of the pain she felt.

He finally broke for air, and grinned down at her. "Who would have thought it?"

"I know." Robyn smiled back at him. He was her hero.

Jeff managed to get his arm around her without touching the slashes in her back, and she snuggled down happily. The pain was still there in her back, her arm, her hand, and her lungs. But they would go. "You know," she said thoughtfully, "it's really weird, isn't it?"

"Well, Joe Butler planned on killing a Leo tonight, and he did. Himself."

"Bizarre," agreed Jeff. "But the Zodiac killer stops there. It's all over now."

"Yes," Debi said. She coughed, but she was getting over her near-drowning. "Jeff, I owe you an apology for making Robyn doubt you. I'm sorry."

"It's okay," he said. "I guess I do behave a little— differently from time to time. But I'm not used to having people around to share things with. Maybe I'll do better from now on." He stuck his hand out. "Friends?"

"Friends," Debi agreed, slapping his palm. Then, stung by some inner devil, she couldn't resist adding, "But I'm astonished it took us so long to realize who the real killer was. After all, in all the mystery clichés, it's always the Butler that did it."

Jeff groaned.

Robyn just grinned weakly. She felt pretty dreadful and pretty good at the same time. She hurt all over, but the killer was dead, and they were all still alive. And she hadn't made the wrong choice about Jeff. All in all, she felt pretty lucky.

She looked upward at the sky for the first time that evening. There were hundreds of stars. Whether or not they influenced human lives, they were always a wonderful sight to see. Especially since she had thought she'd never live to see them again.

People lived, died, and loved—and the stars watched over them.

AUTHOR'S NOTE

The Society for Creative Anachronism is a real group. It's organized pretty much along the lines I use here, though I have taken one or two liberties. If it sounds like the kind of thing you'd like to join, the reference librarian at your local public library will be happy to give you further information on the S.C.A., and an address to write to if you want to get involved.

I'd like to thank my own contacts in the S.C.A. for some most enjoyable times. Especially John and Fern Francavillo, who introduced me to this alternative reality, and to Rusty Young, the world's largest leprechaun.